A **NORMA** AND **BELLY** BOOK

PIZZA
MY HEART

This book was drawn with pencils, sumi brushes, sumi ink, and watercolors on watercolor paper.

Text, cover art, and interior illustrations copyright © 2022 by Mika Song

All rights reserved. Published in the United States by RH Graphic, an imprint of Random House Children's Books, a division of Penguin Random House LLC, New York.

RH Graphic with the book design is a trademark of Penguin Random House LLC.

Visit us on the web and sign up for our newsletter! RHKidsGraphic.com • @RHKidsGraphic

Educators and librarians, for a variety of teaching tools, visit us at RHTeachersLibrarians.com

Library of Congress Cataloging-in-Publication Data is available upon request.
ISBN 978-0-593-47972-8 (hardcover) — ISBN 978-0-593-47973-5 (lib. bdg.)
ISBN 978-0-593-47974-2 (ebook)

Designed by Patrick Crotty

MANUFACTURED IN CHINA
10 9 8 7 6 5 4 3 2 1
First Edition

A comic on every bookshelf.

A **NORMA** AND **BELLY** BOOK

PIZZA

MY HEART

mika Song

Also by Mika Song

———

Tea with Oliver
Picnic with Oliver

Norma and Belly Books

———

Donut Feed the Squirrels
Apple of My Pie

chapter 1

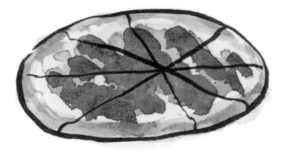

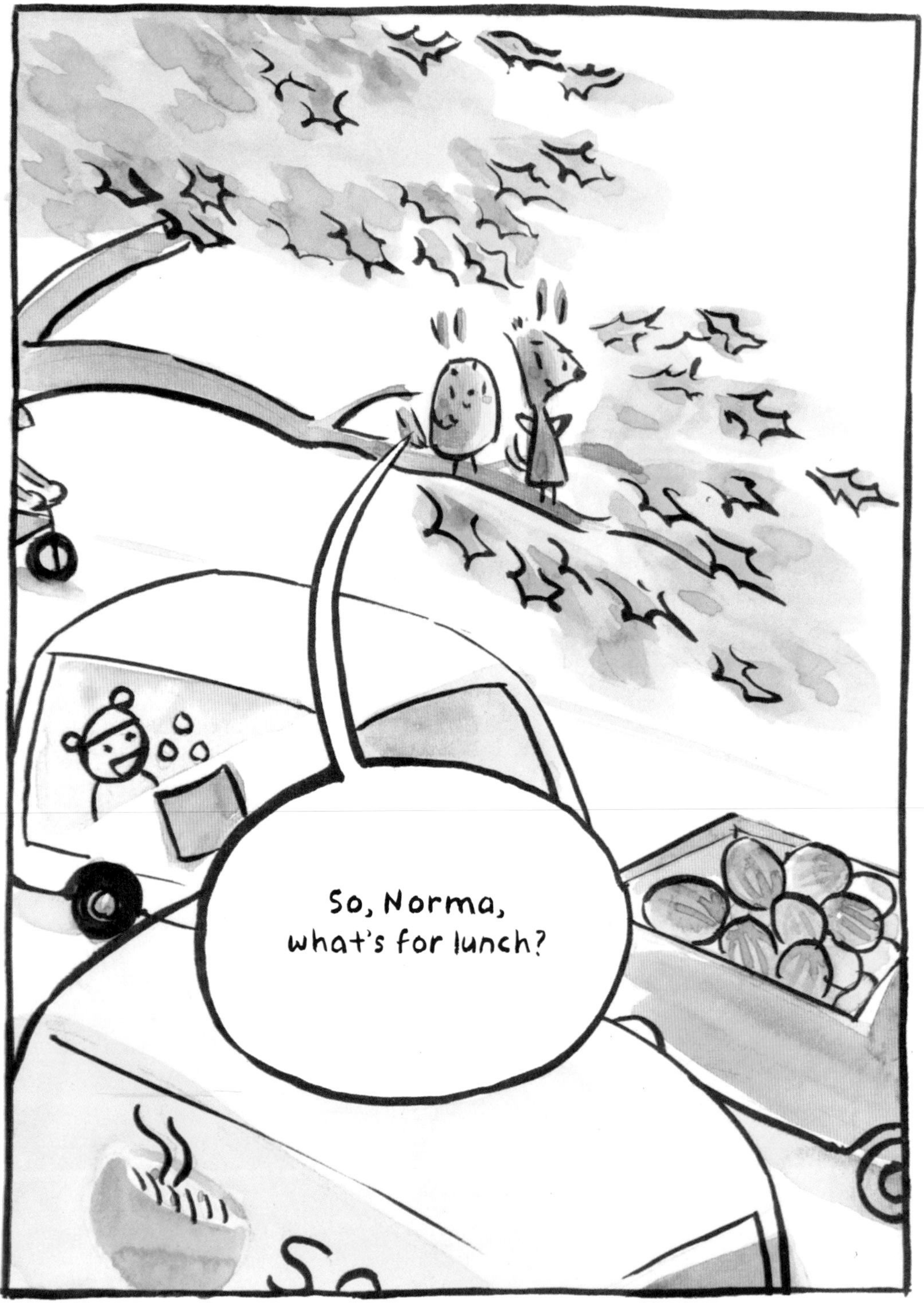
So, Norma, what's for lunch?

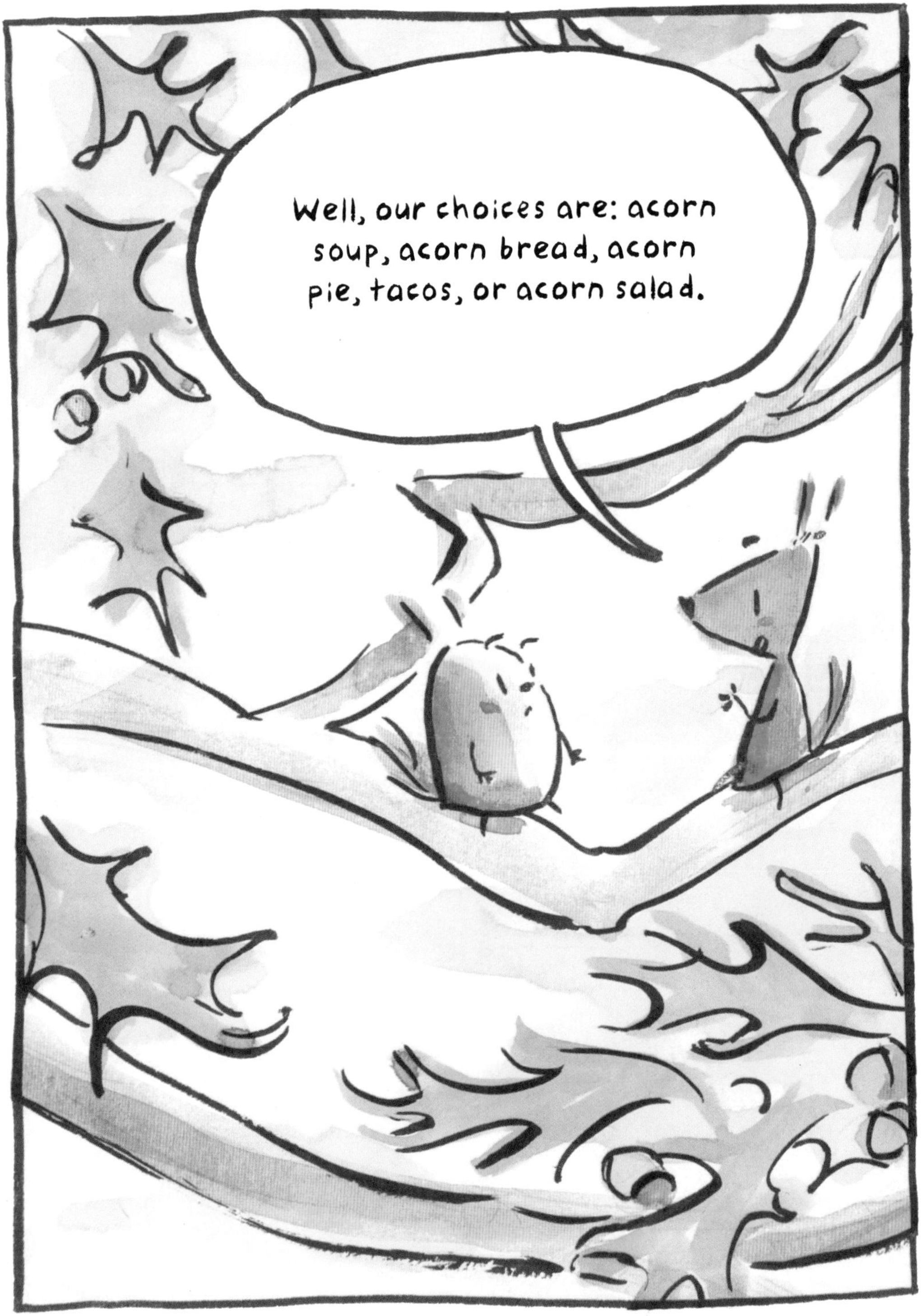
Well, our choices are: acorn soup, acorn bread, acorn pie, tacos, or acorn salad.

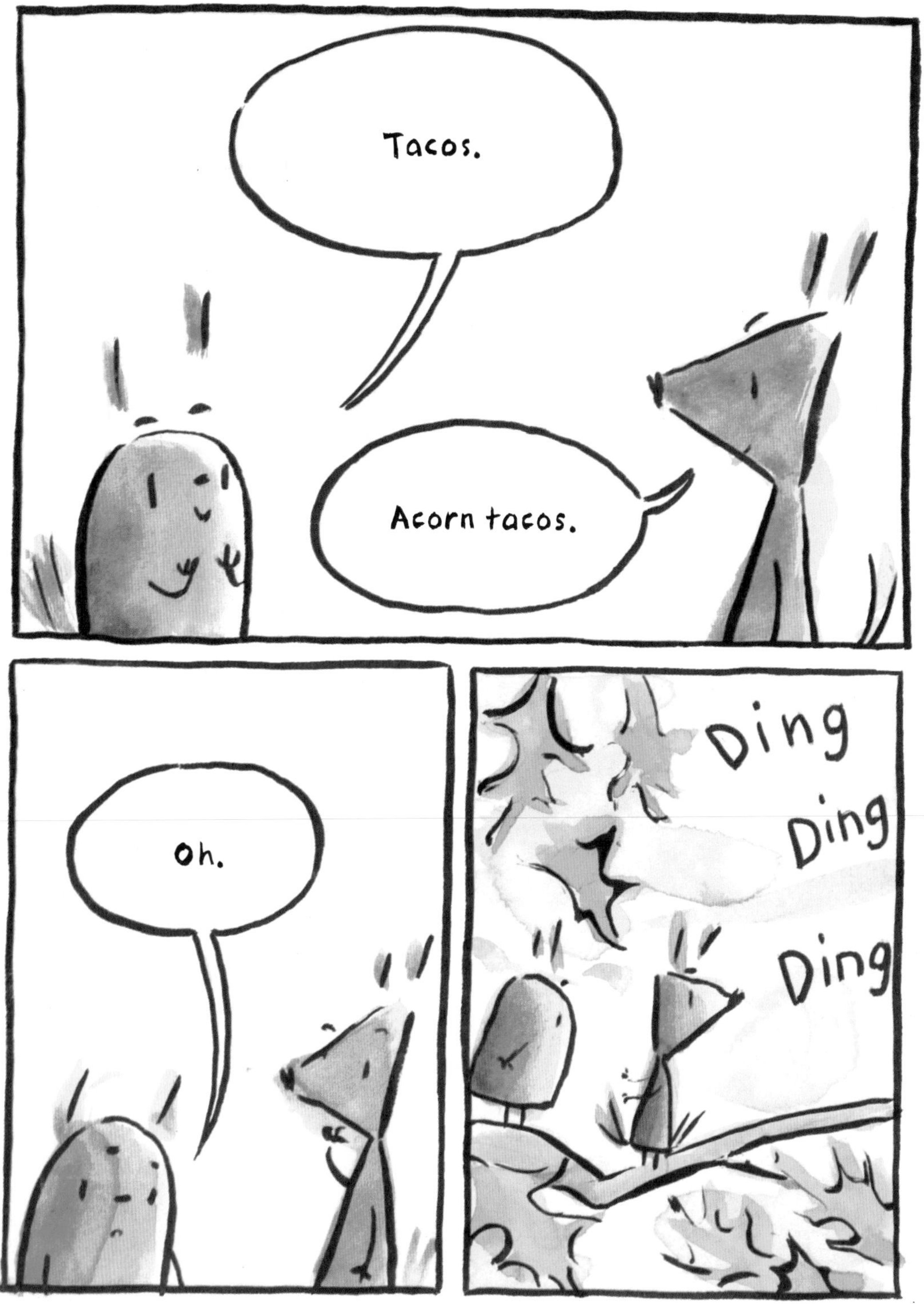
Tacos.
Acorn tacos.
Oh.
Ding
Ding
Ding

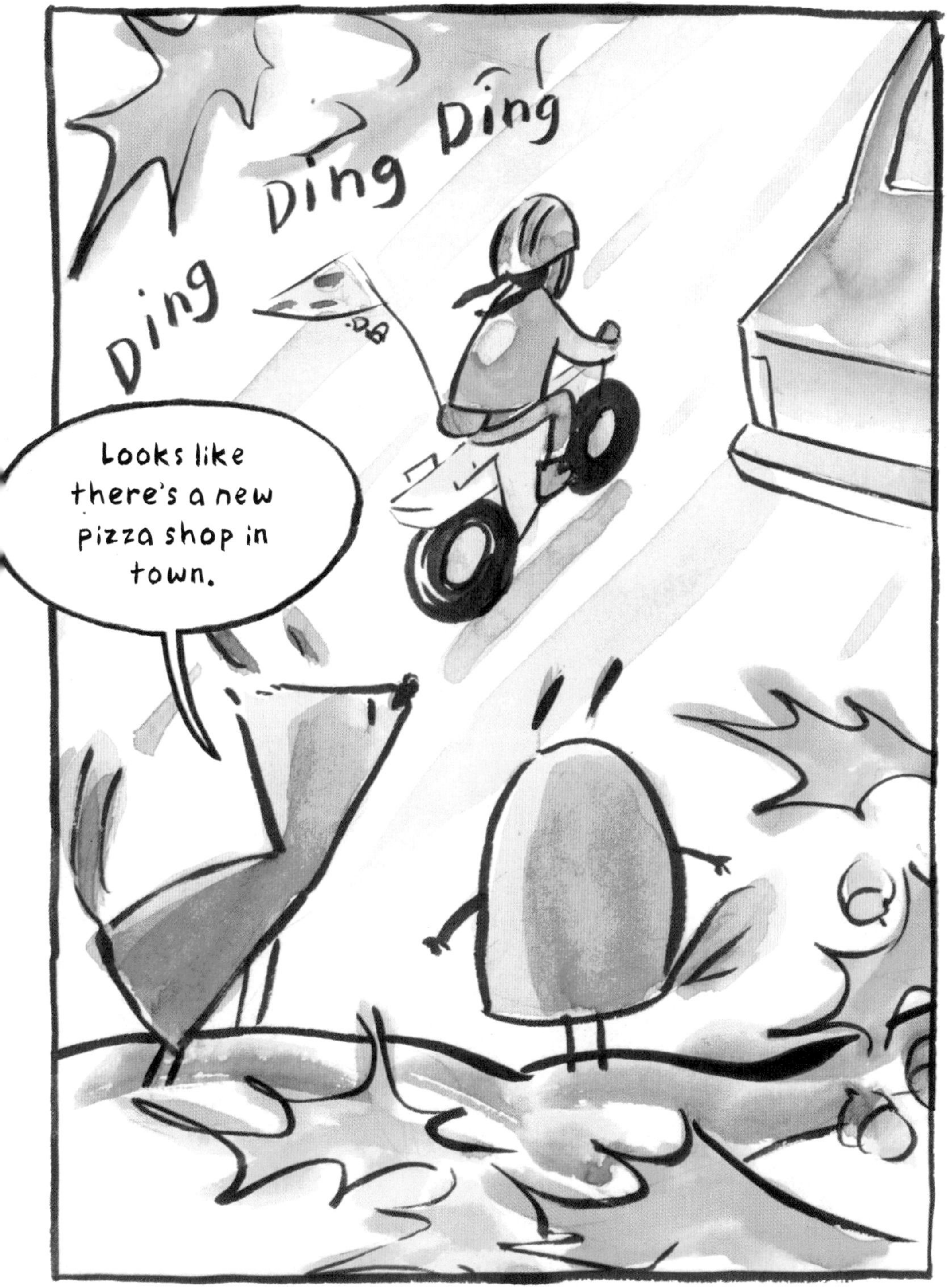
Ding Ding Ding
Looks like there's a new pizza shop in town.

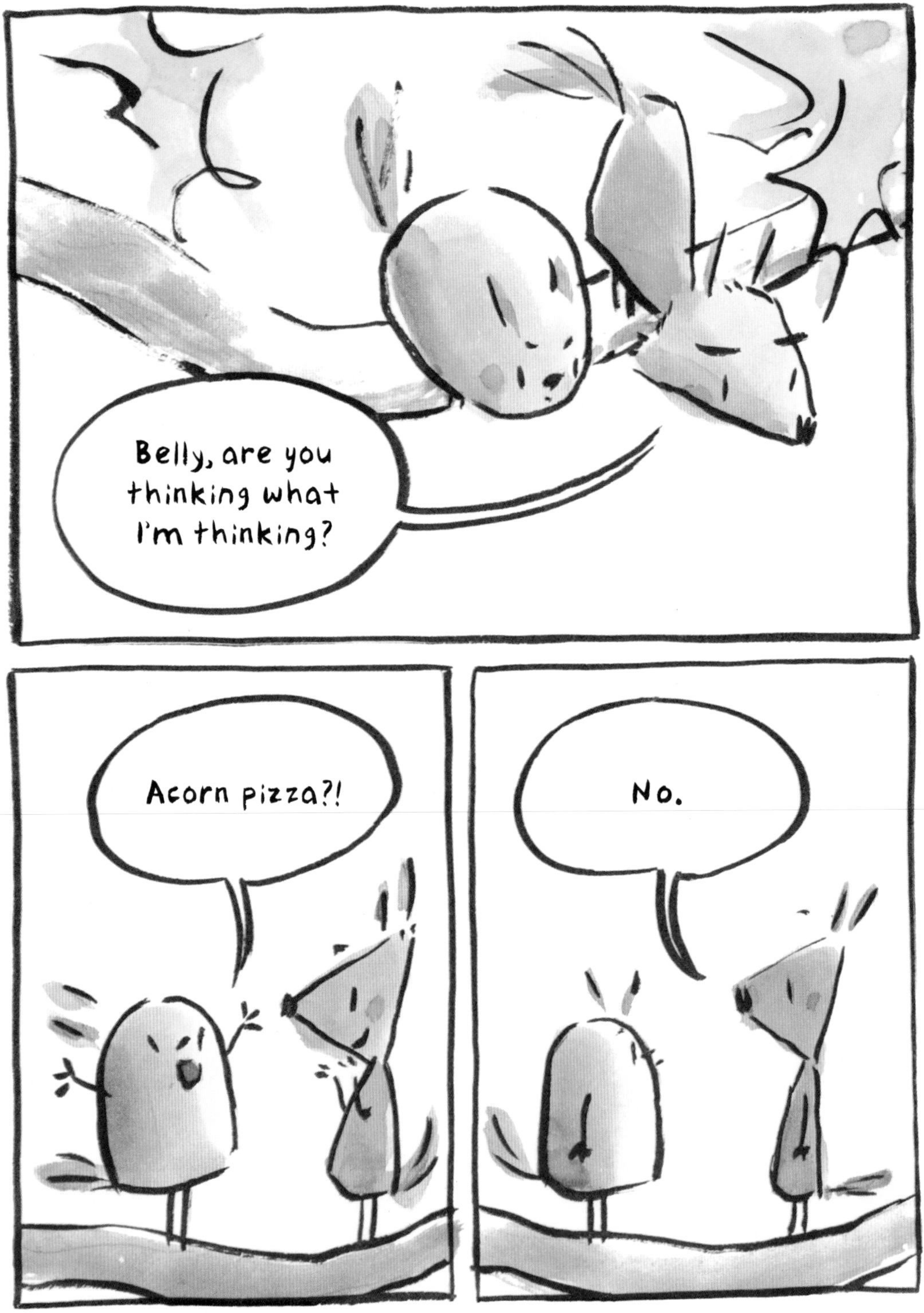
Belly, are you thinking what I'm thinking?
Acorn pizza?!
No.

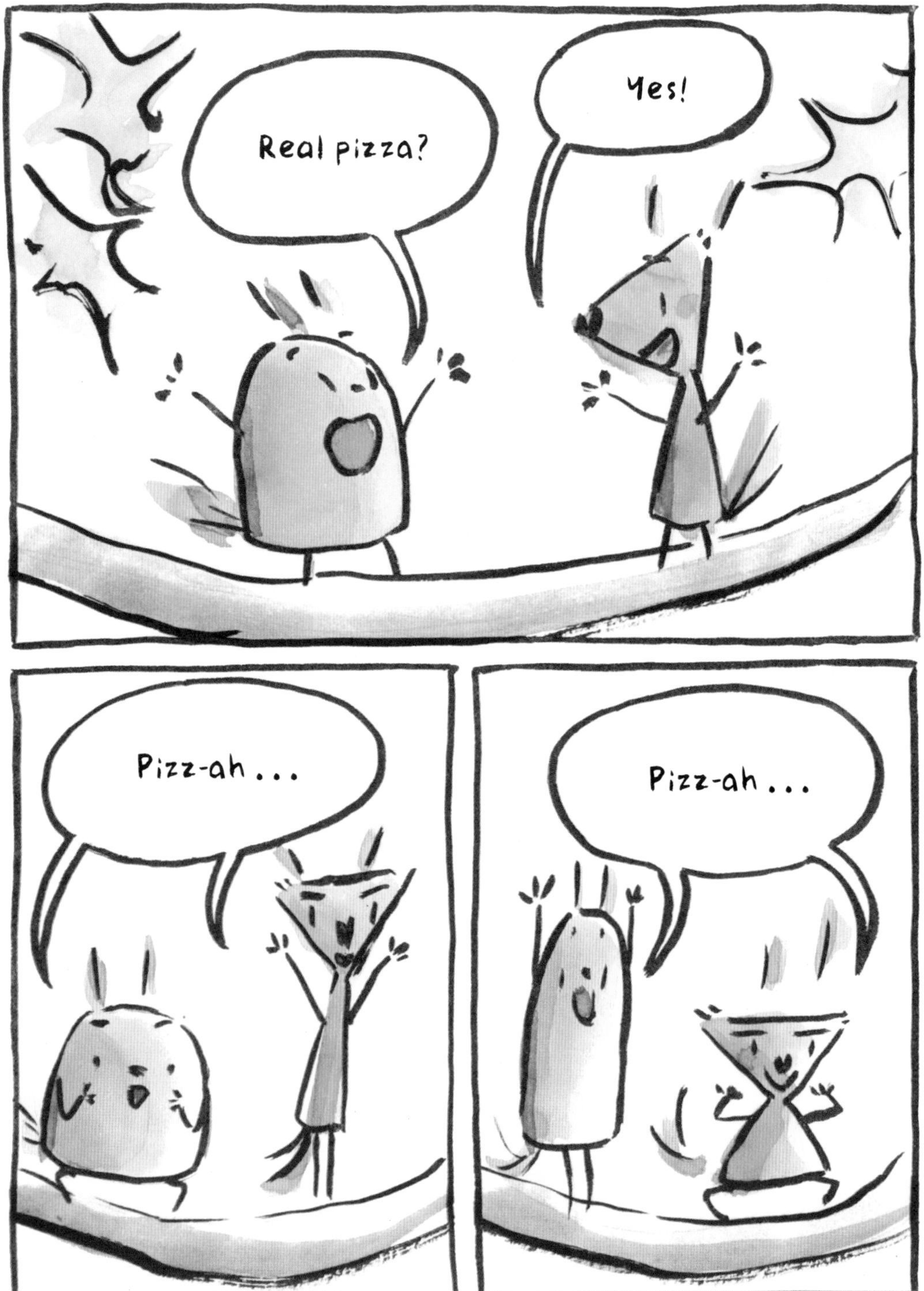
Real pizza?
Yes!
Pizz-ah...
Pizz-ah...

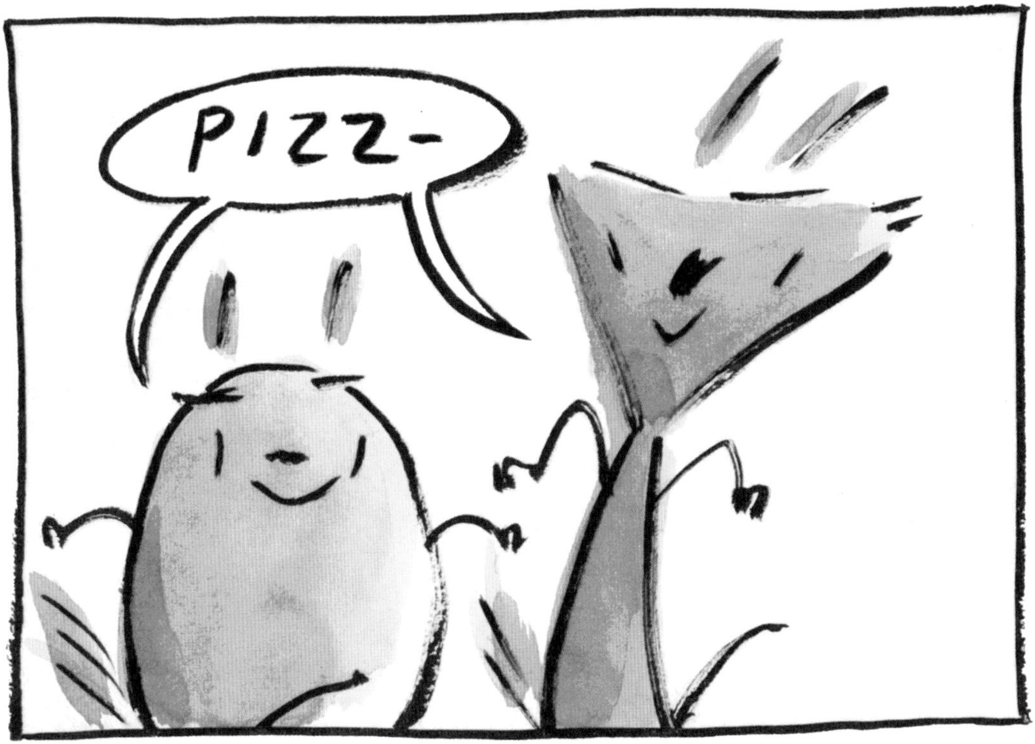
PIZZ-

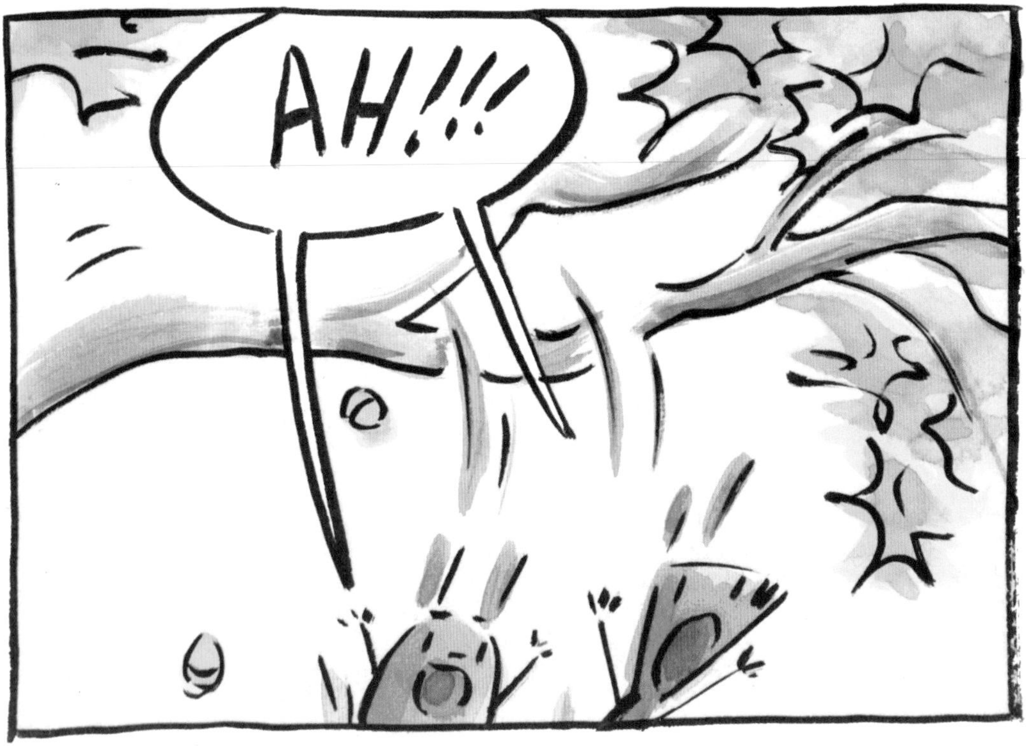
AH!!!

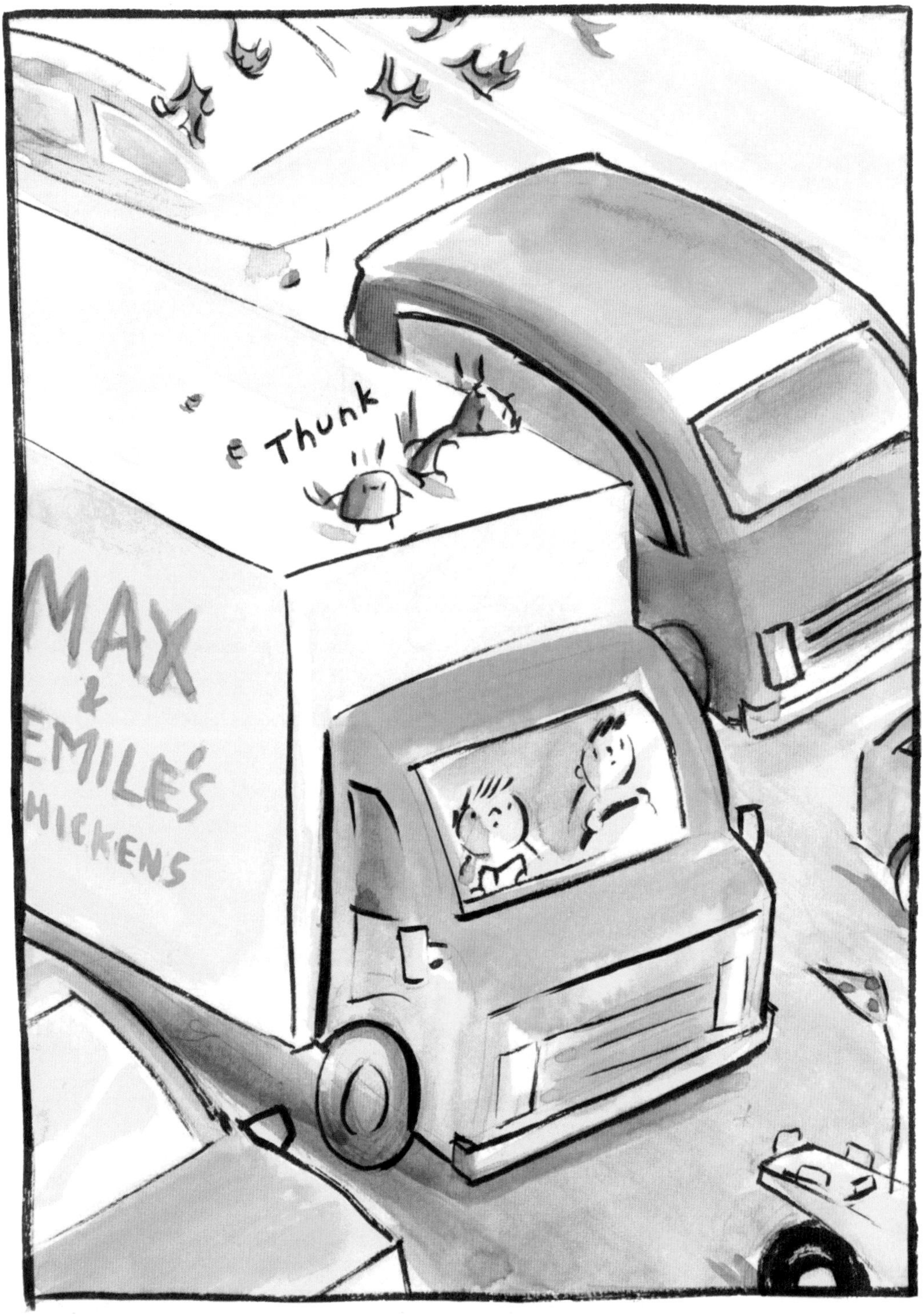
Thunk
MAX
&
EMILE'S
CHICKENS

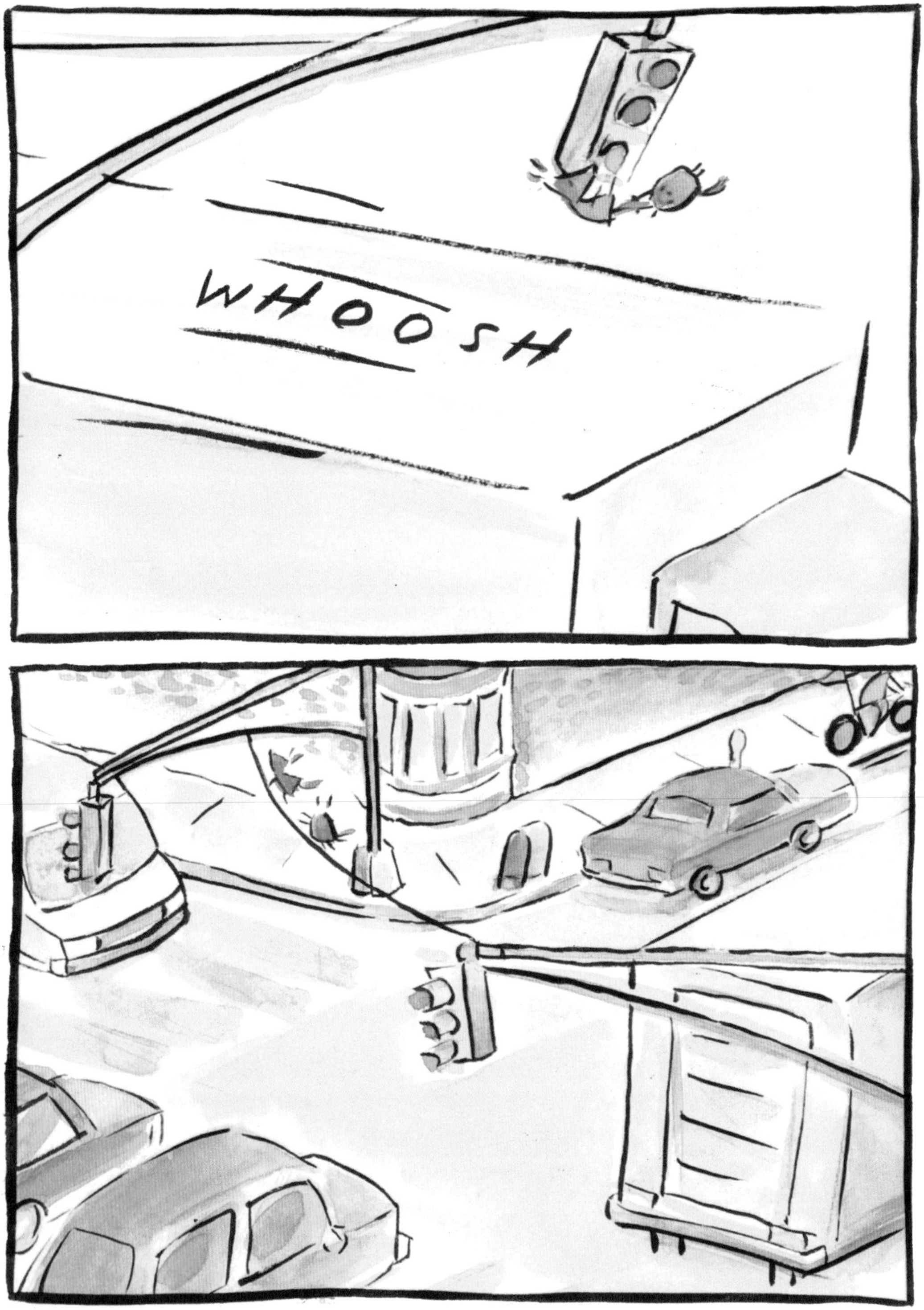
WHOOSH

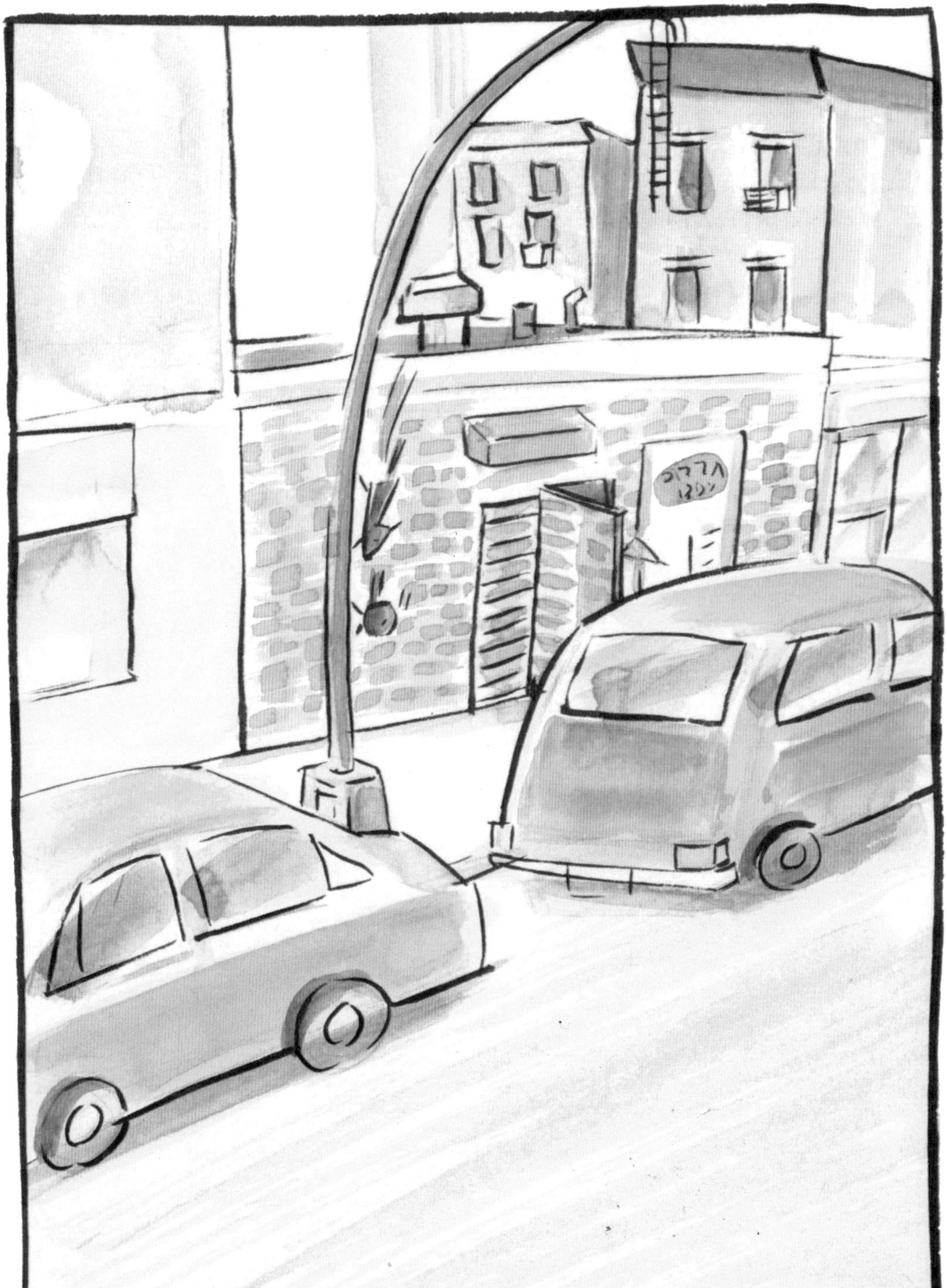

chapter 2

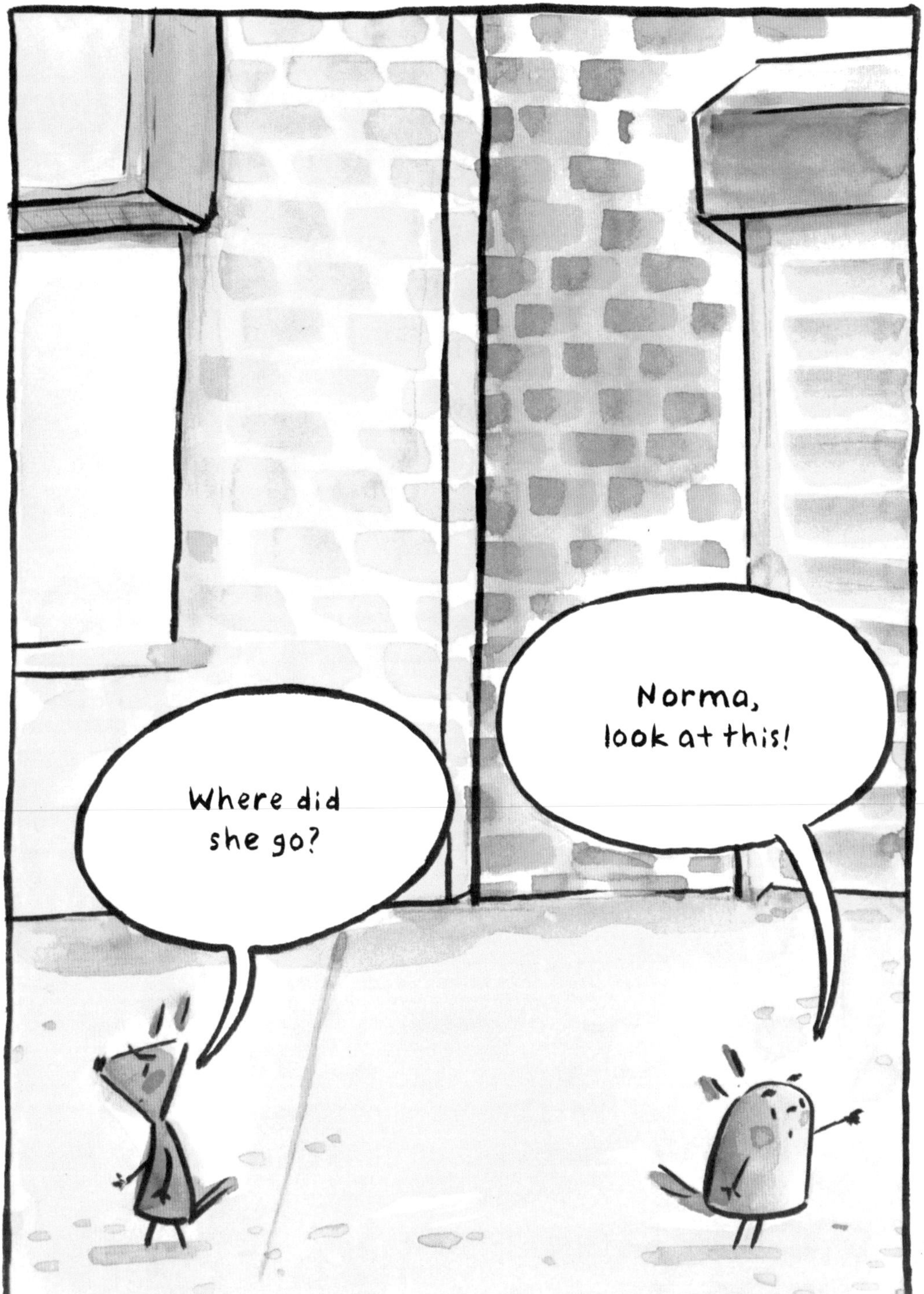
Where did she go?
Norma, look at this!

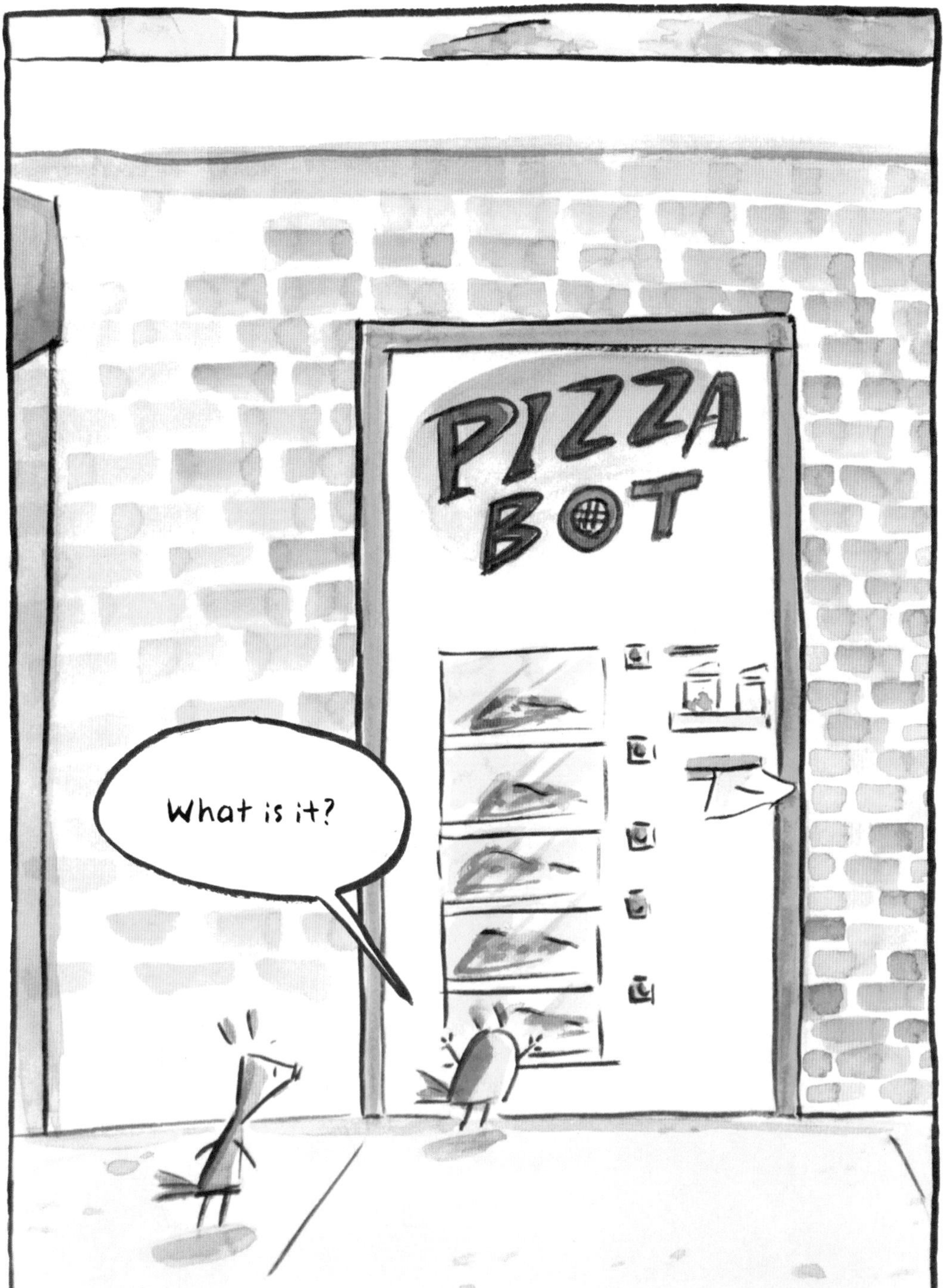
PIZZA BOT
What is it?

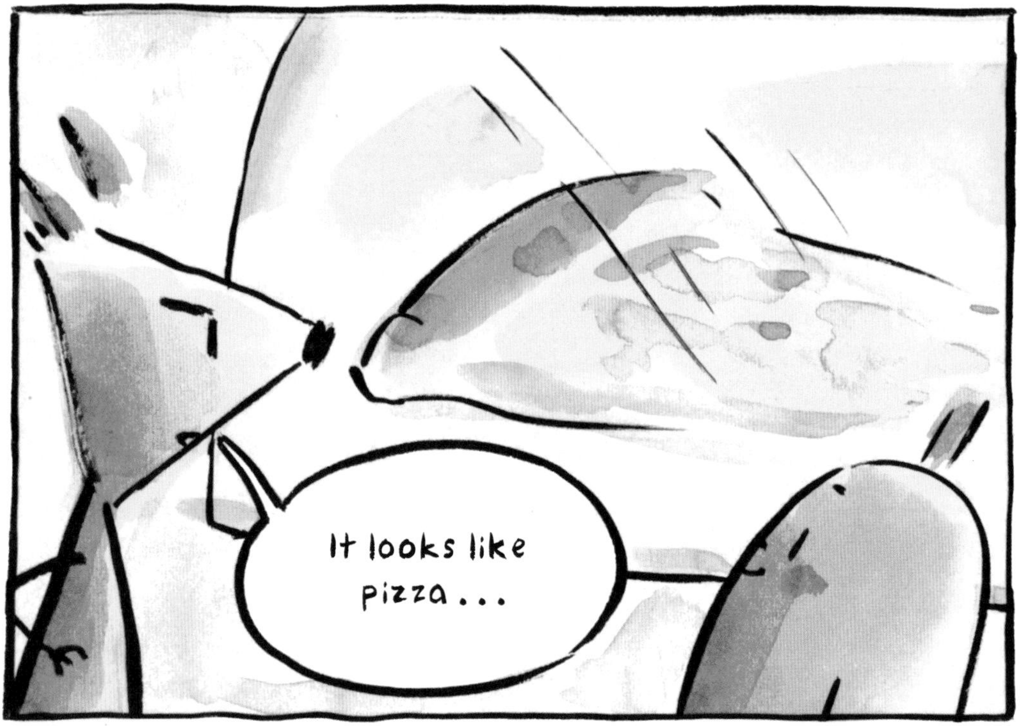
It looks like pizza...

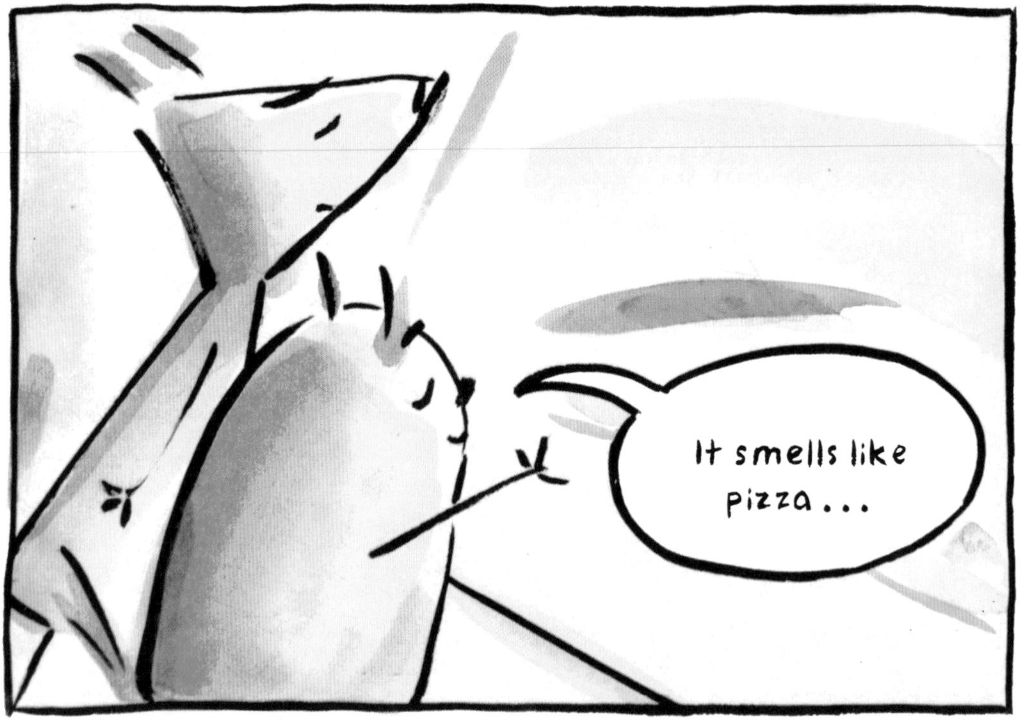
It smells like pizza...

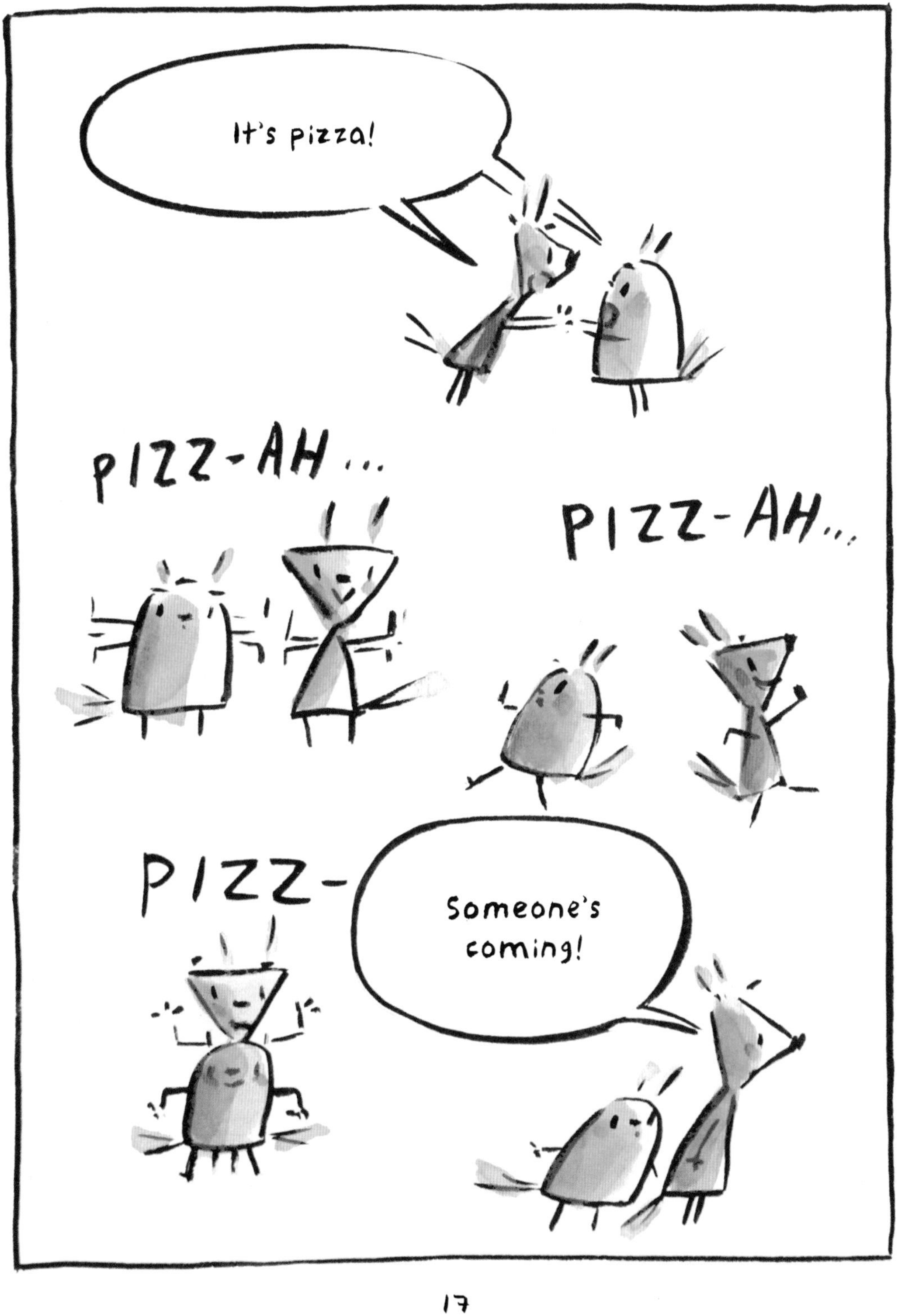
It's pizza!
PIZZ-AH...
PIZZ-AH...
PIZZ-
Someone's coming!

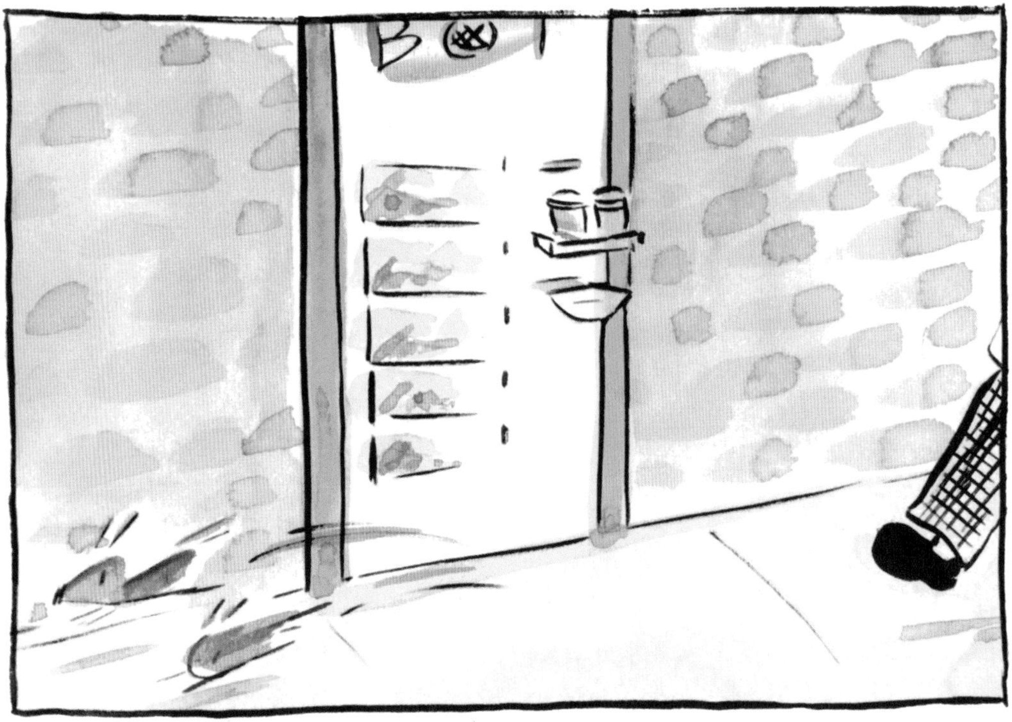

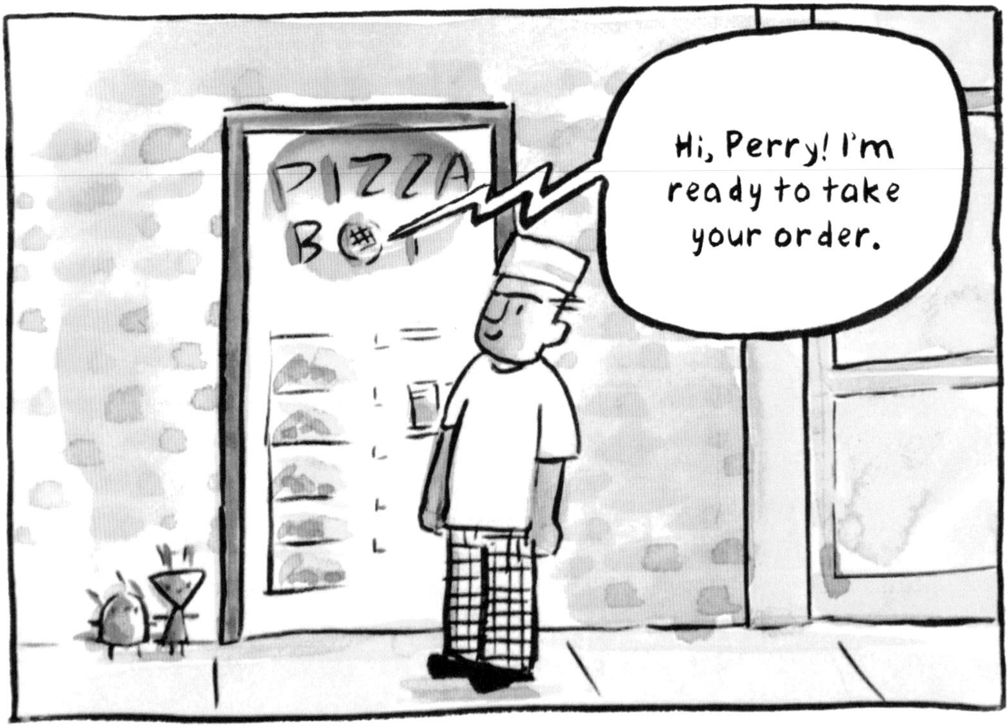
PIZZA
B
Hi, Perry! I'm ready to take your order.

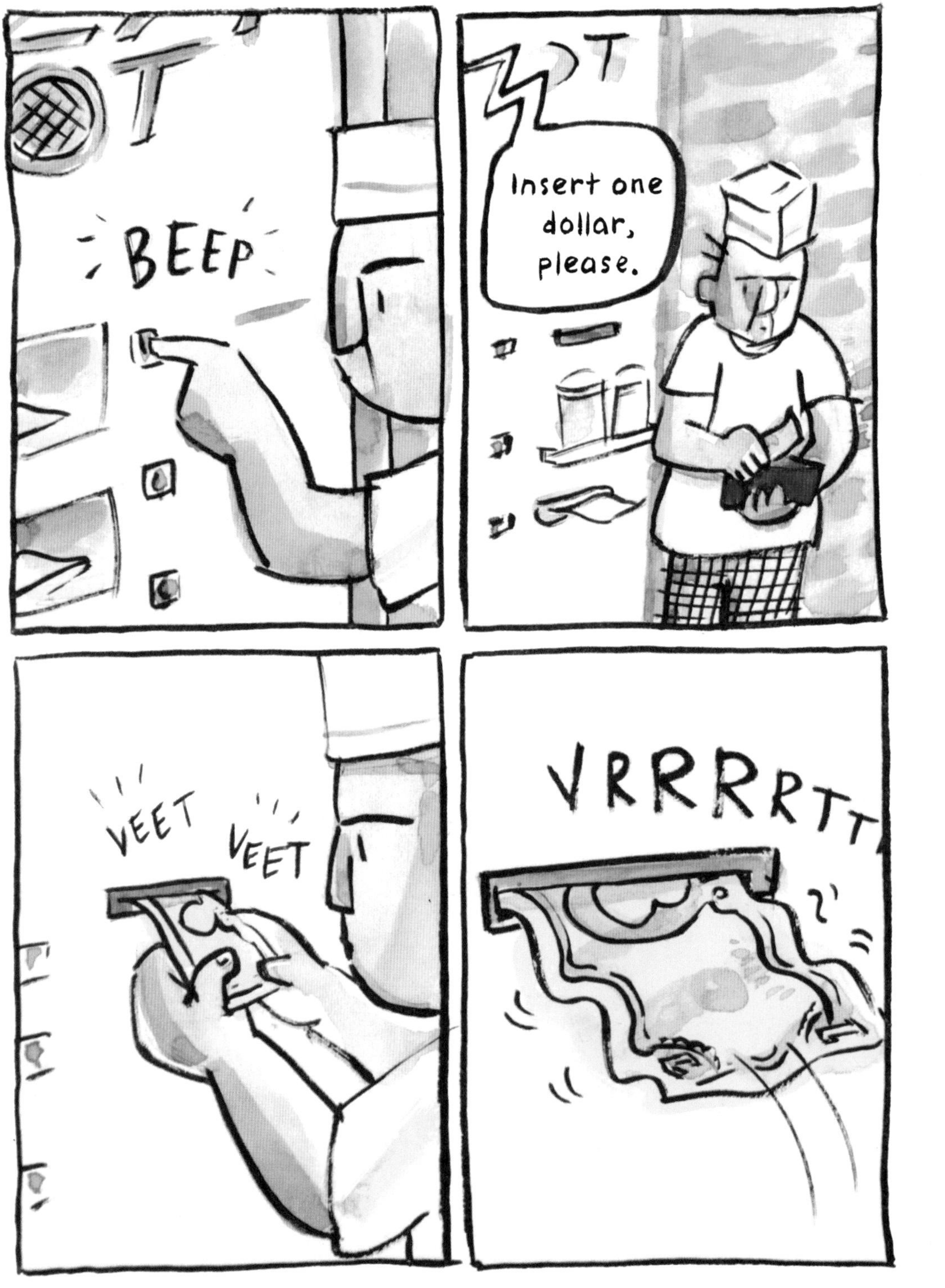
BEEP
Insert one dollar, please.
VEET VEET
VRRRRRTT

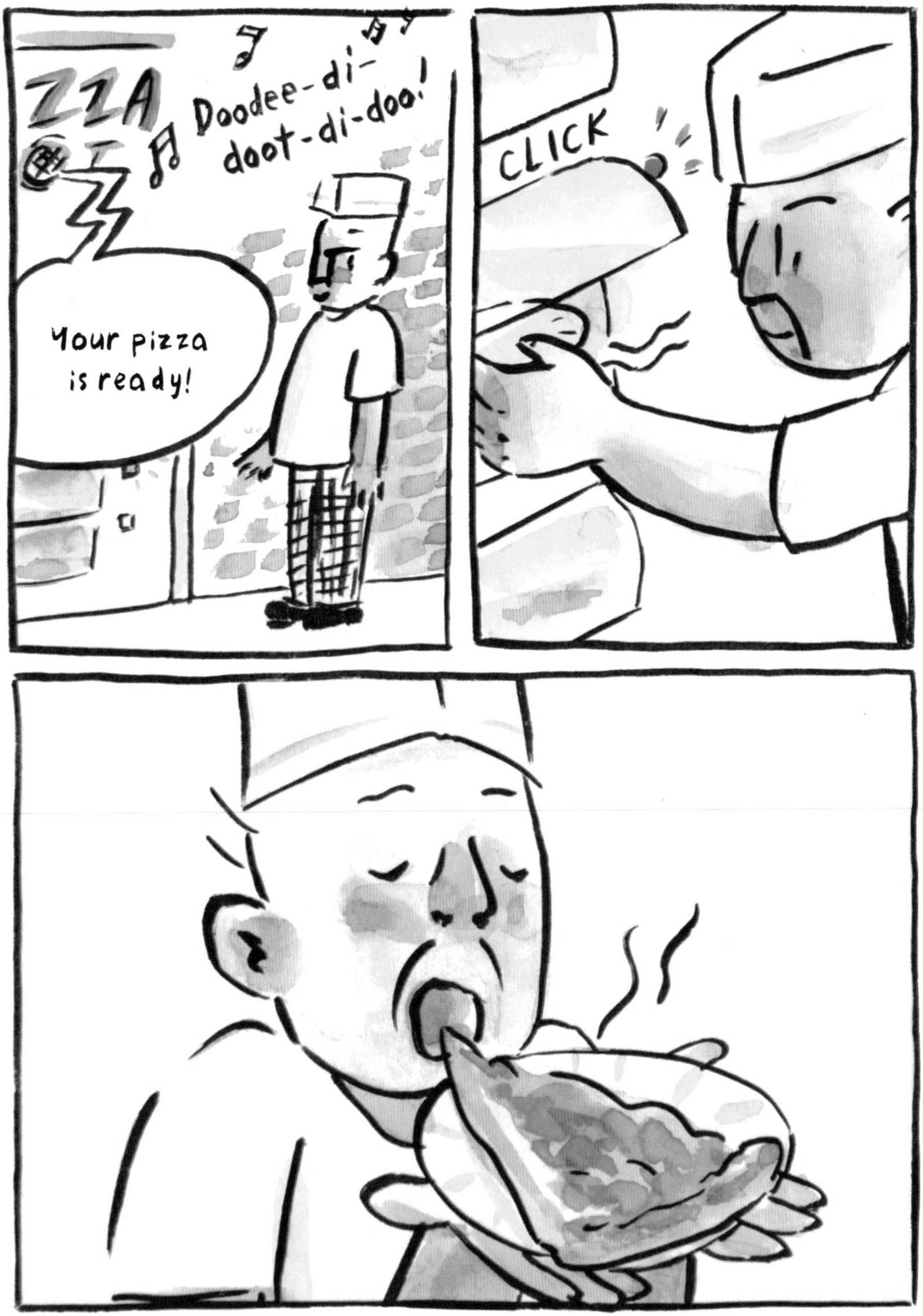
ZZA
Doodee-di-doot-di-doo!
Your pizza is ready!
CLICK

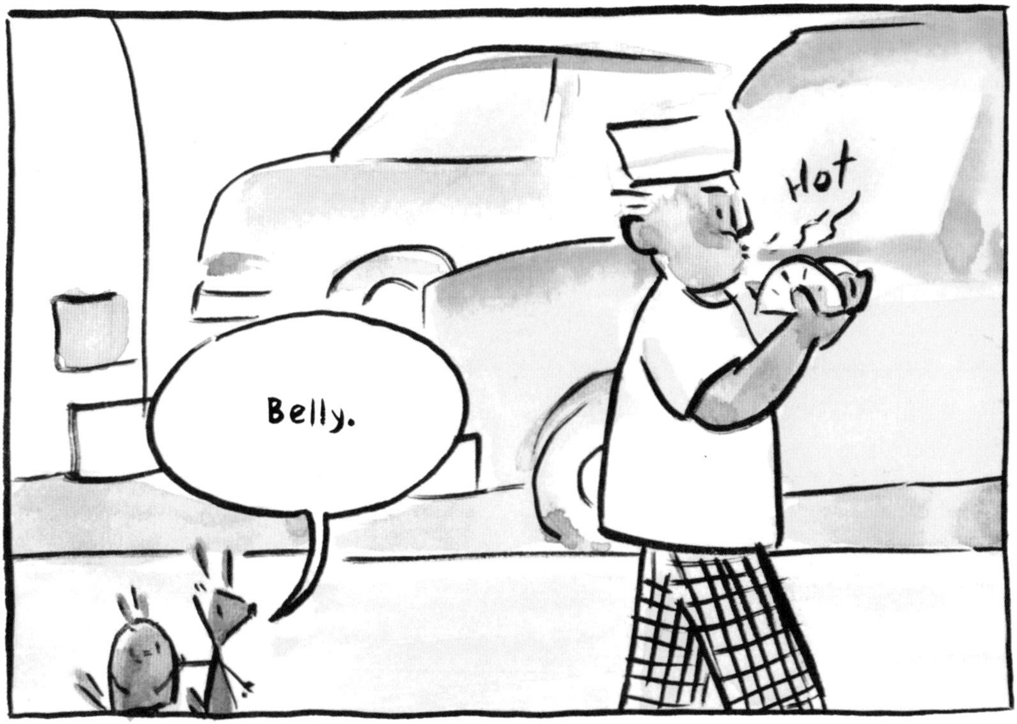
Hot
Belly.

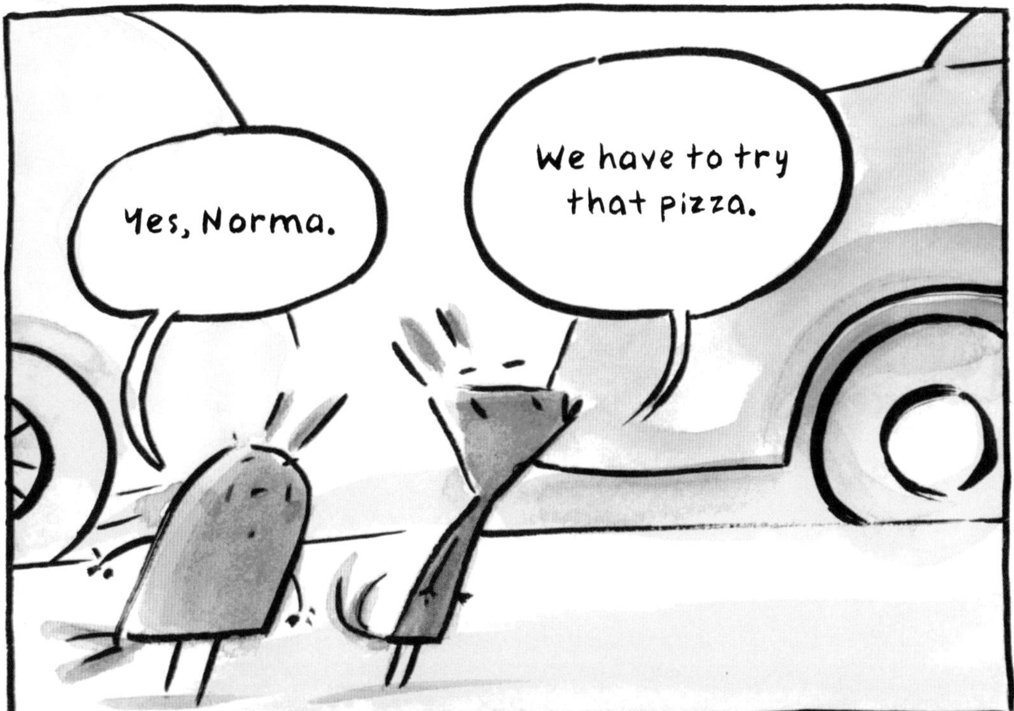
Yes, Norma.
We have to try that pizza.

chapter 3

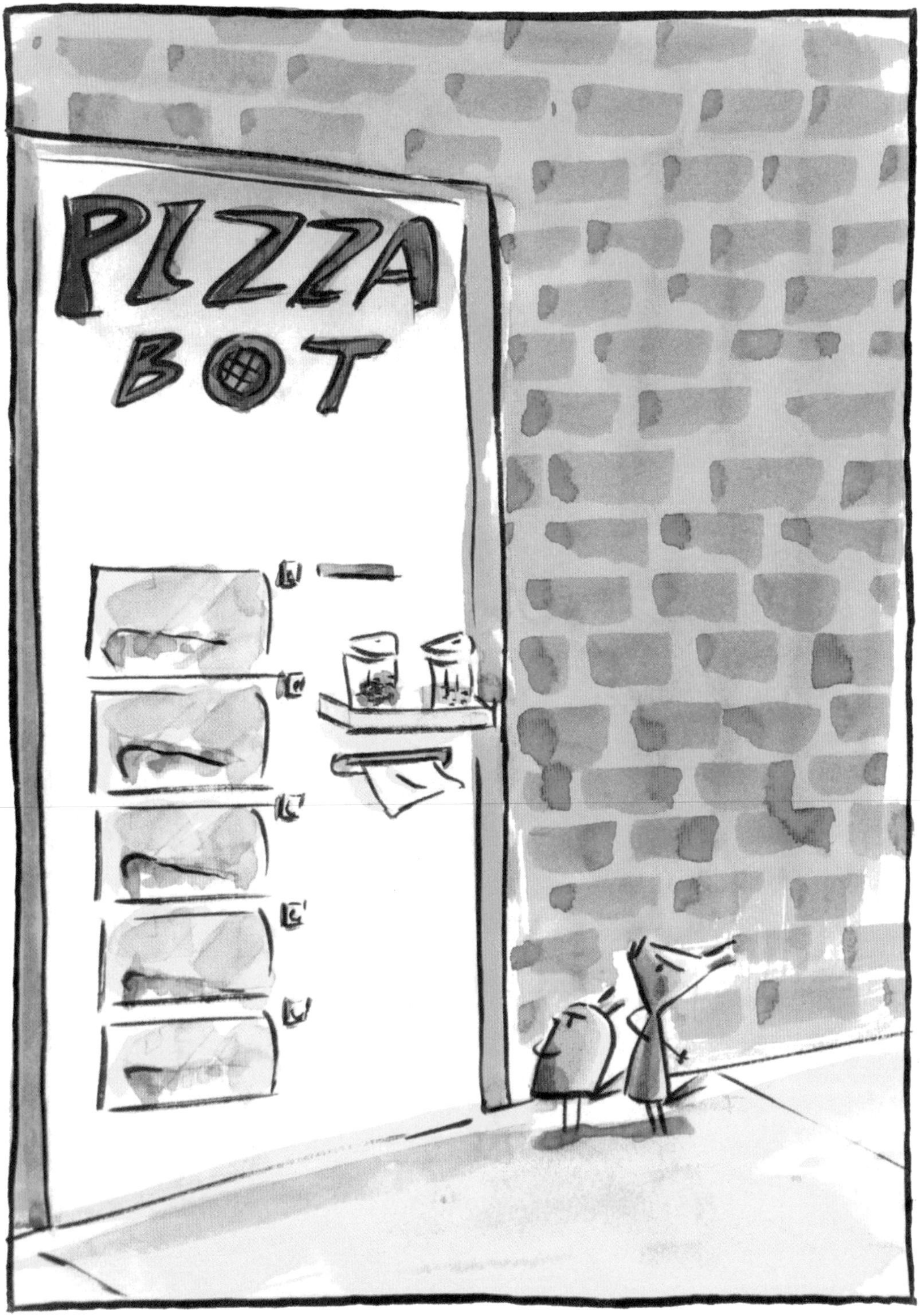
PIZZA
BOT

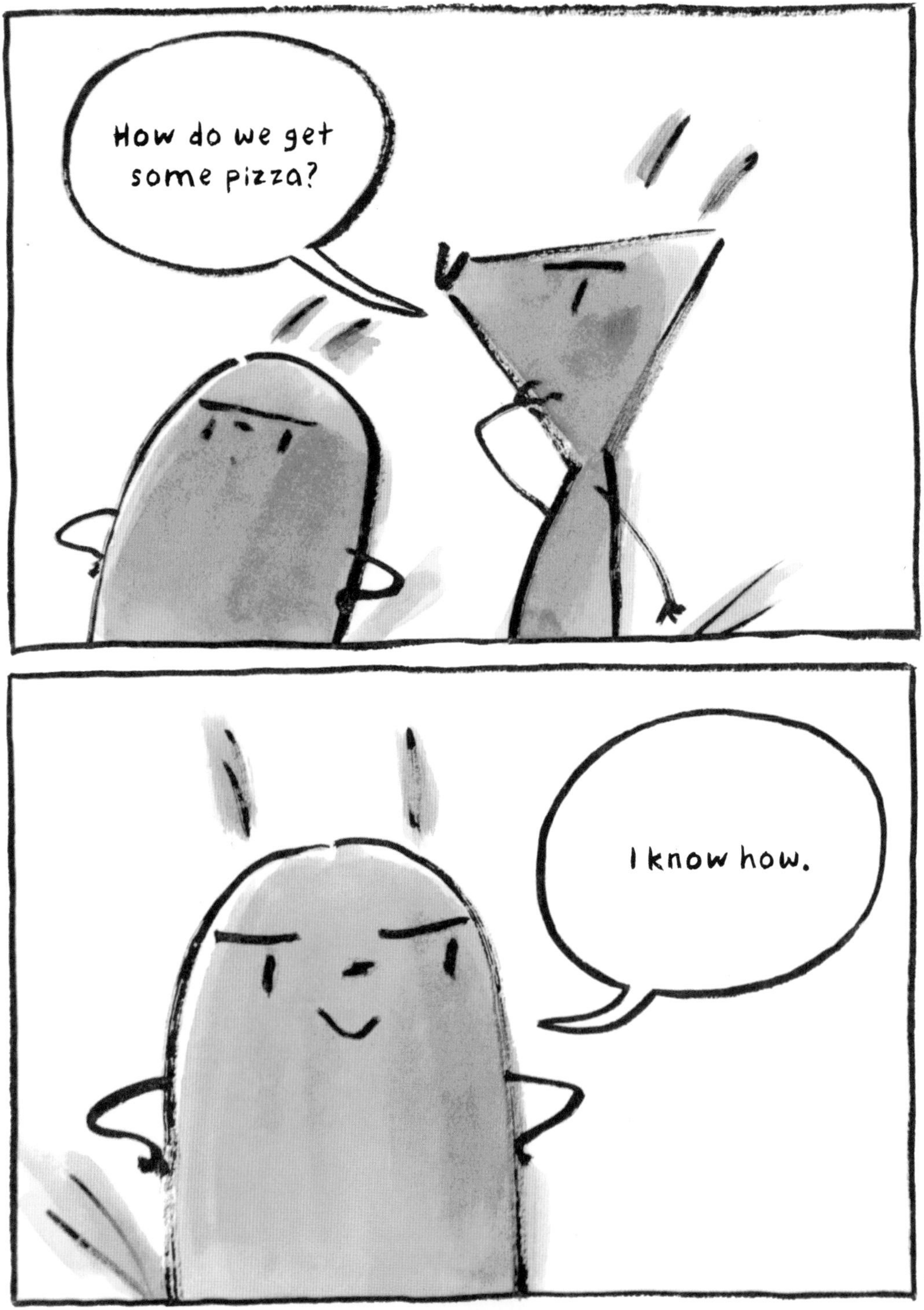
How do we get some pizza?
I know how.

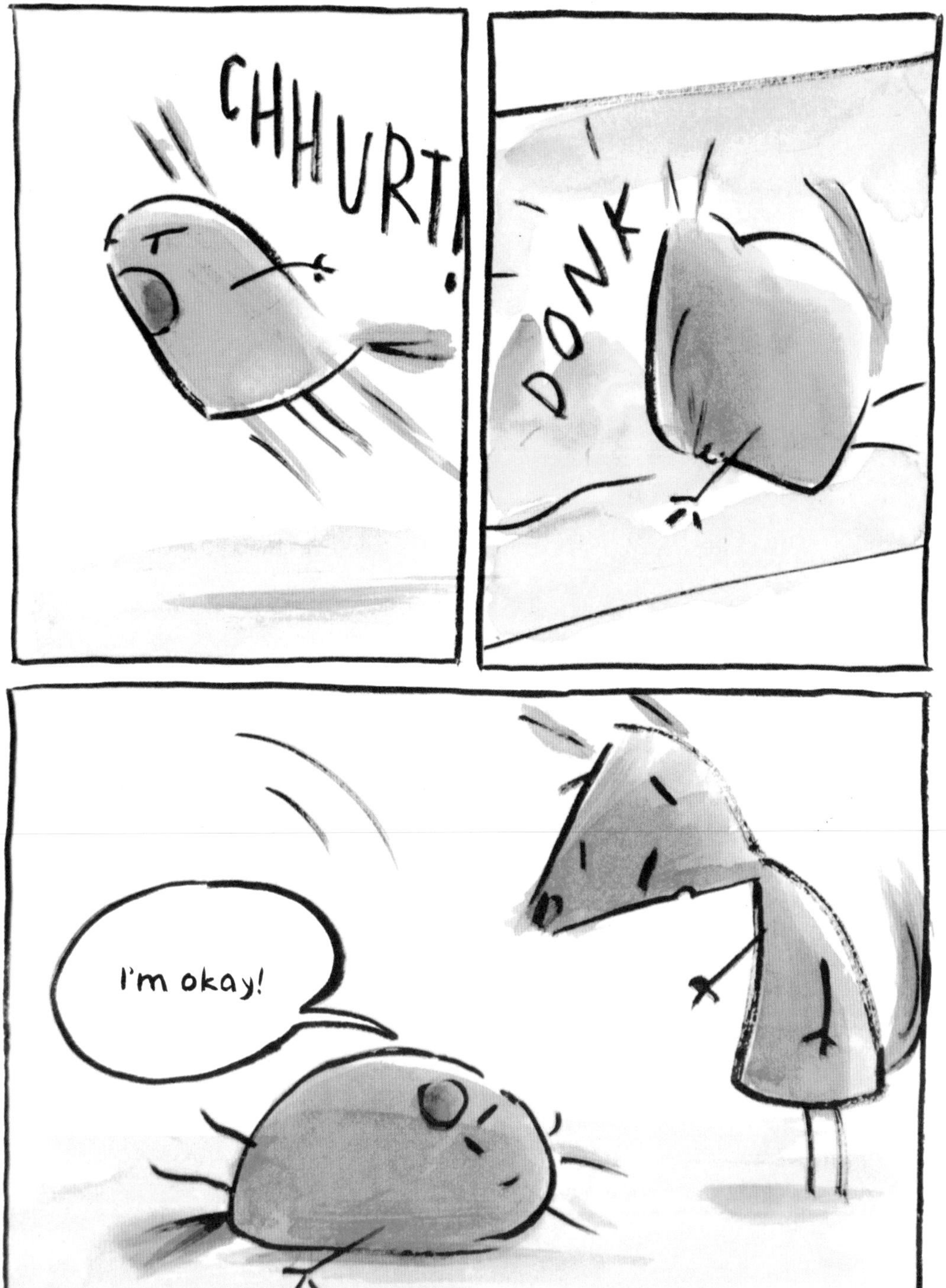
CHHURT!
DONK
I'm okay!

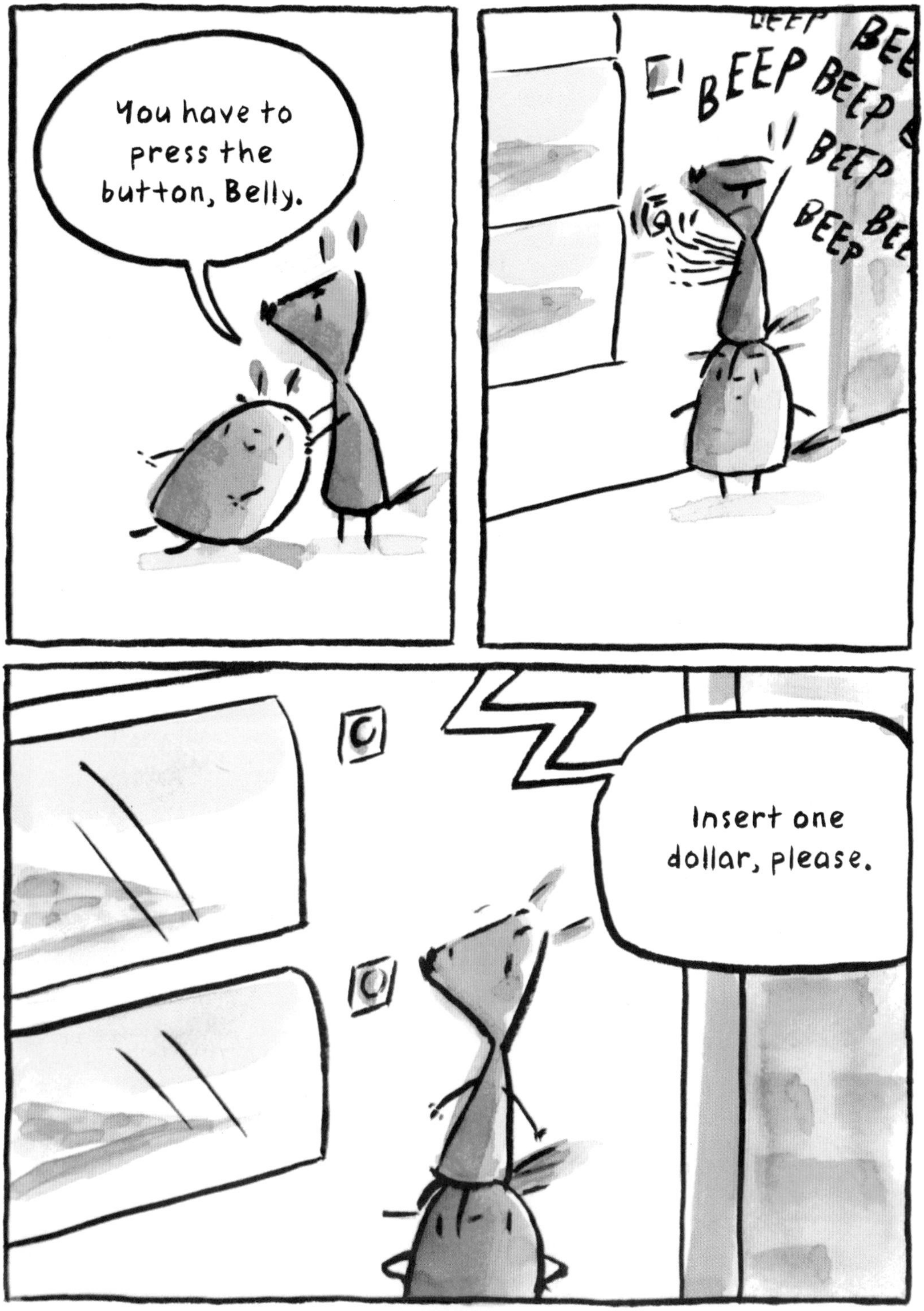
You have to press the button, Belly.
BEEP
BEEP
BEEP
BEEP
Insert one dollar, please.

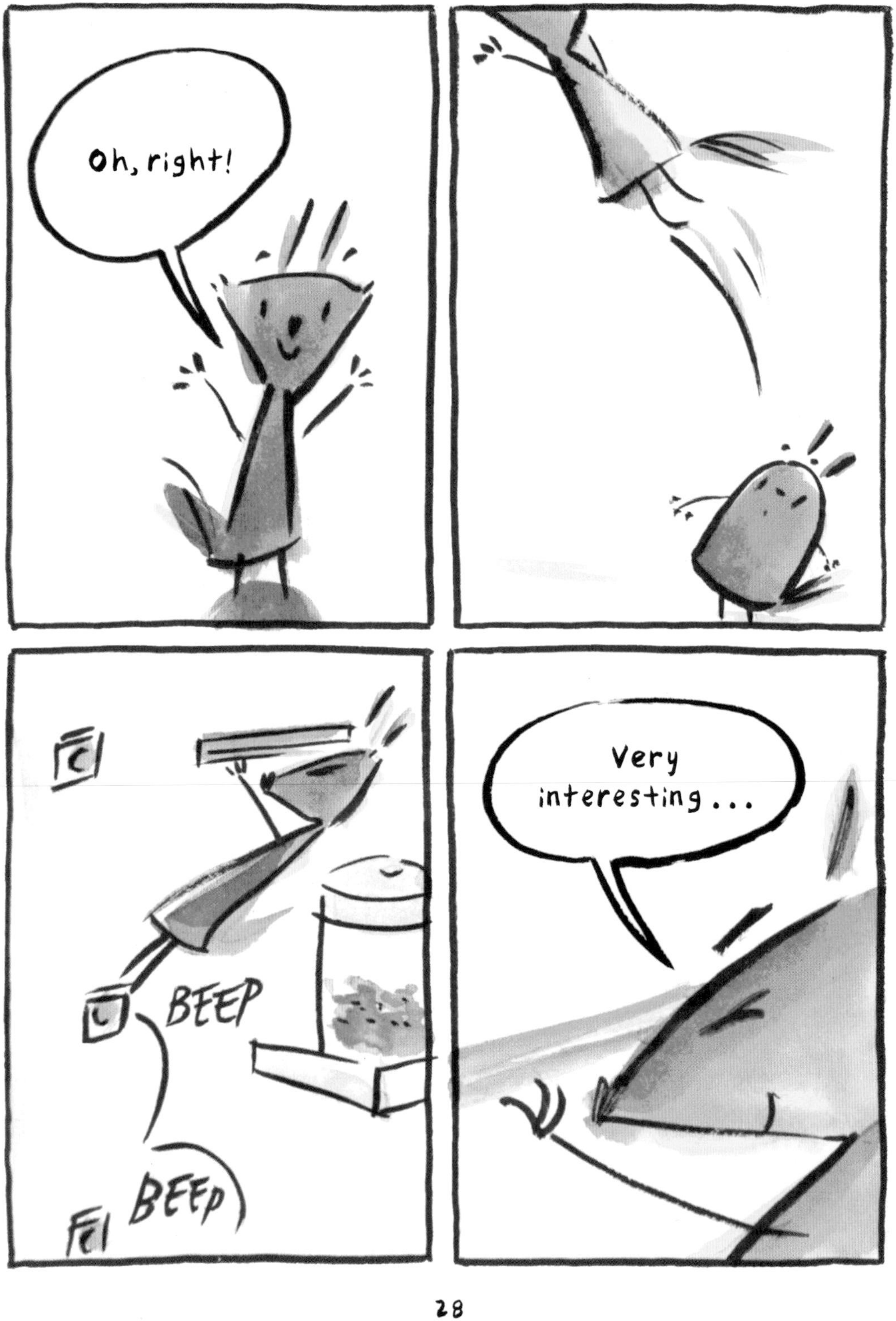
Oh, right!
BEEP
BEEP
Very interesting...

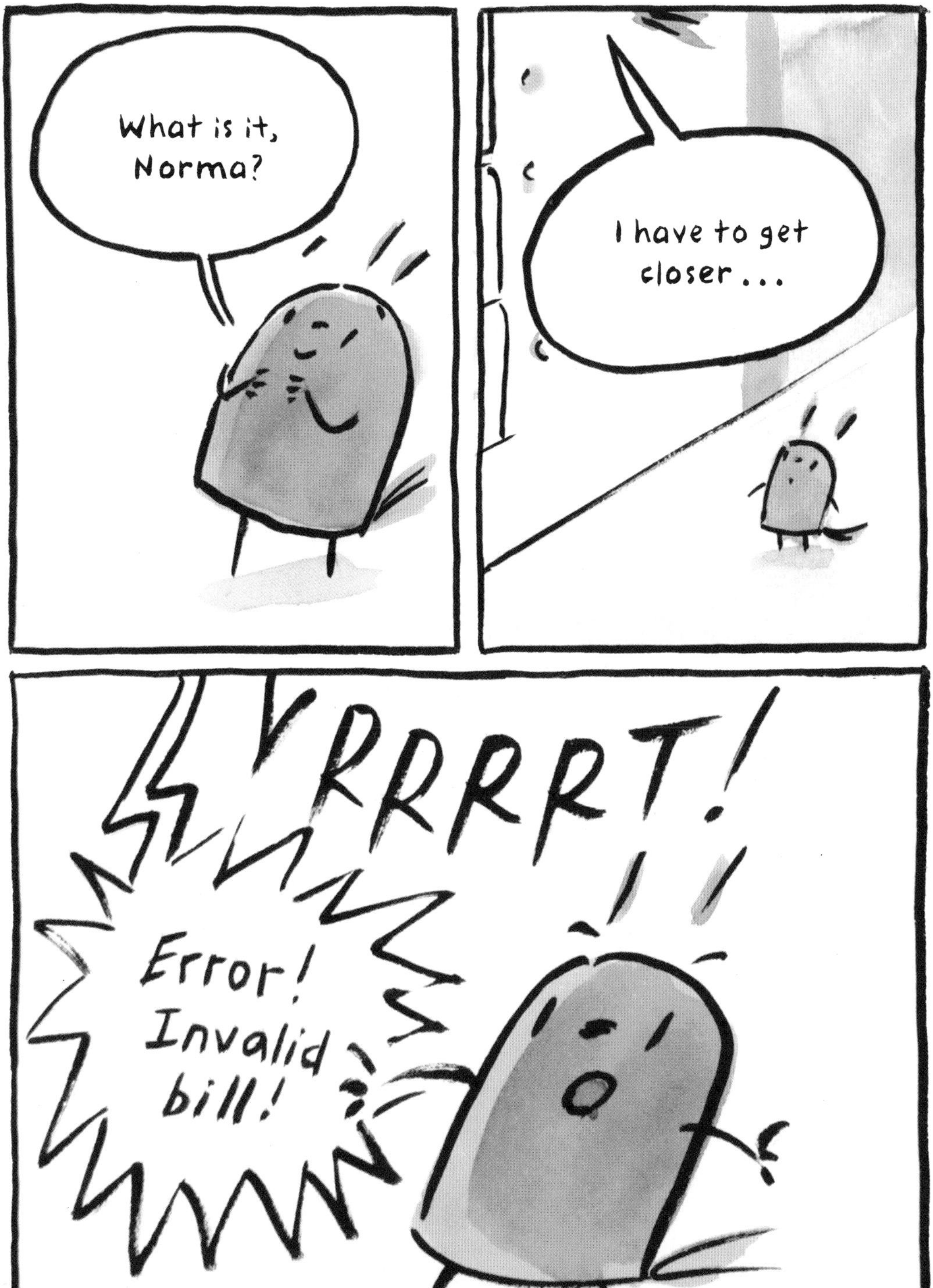
What is it, Norma?
I have to get closer...
RRRRT!
Error! Invalid bill!

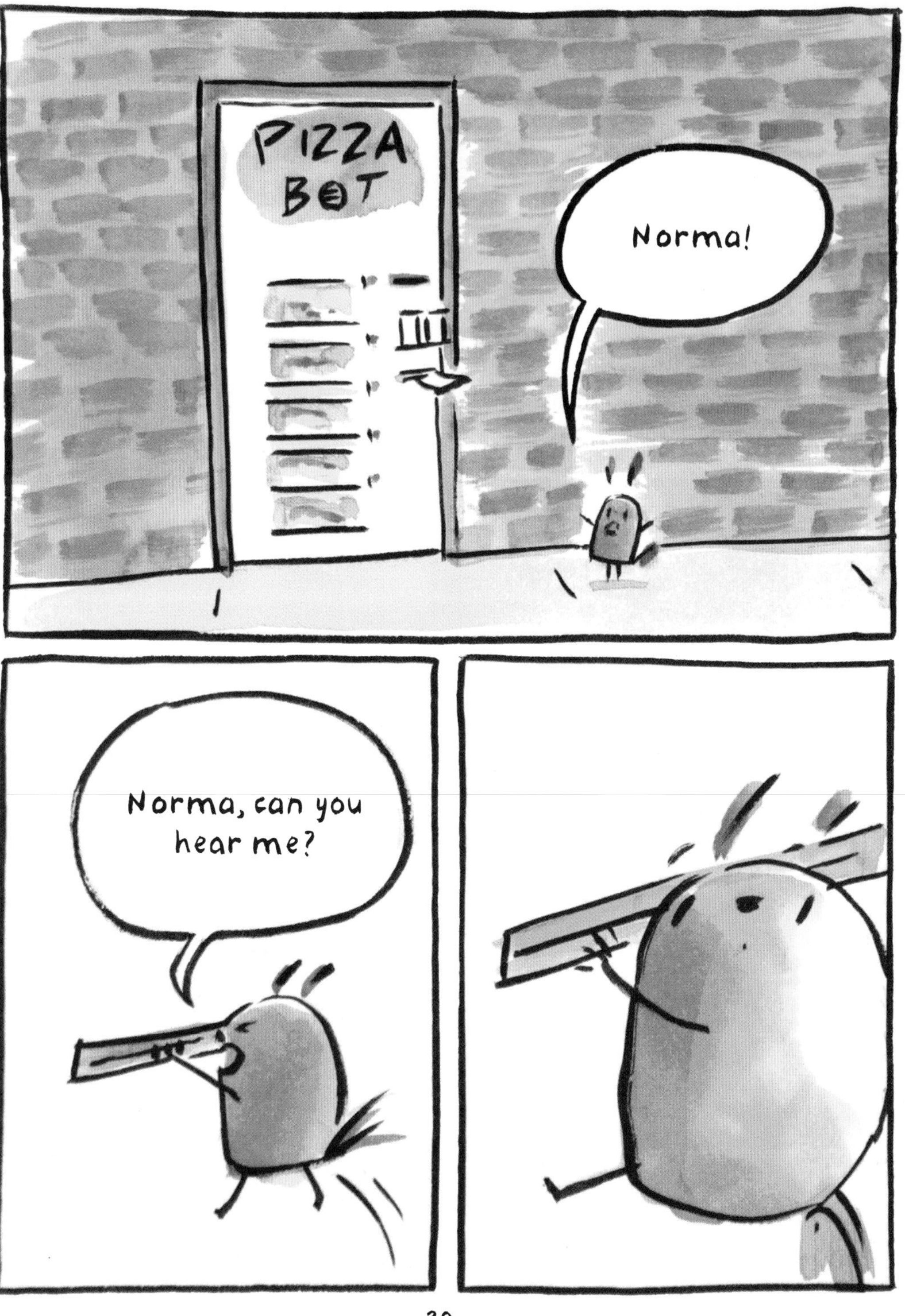
PIZZA BOT
Norma!
Norma, can you hear me?

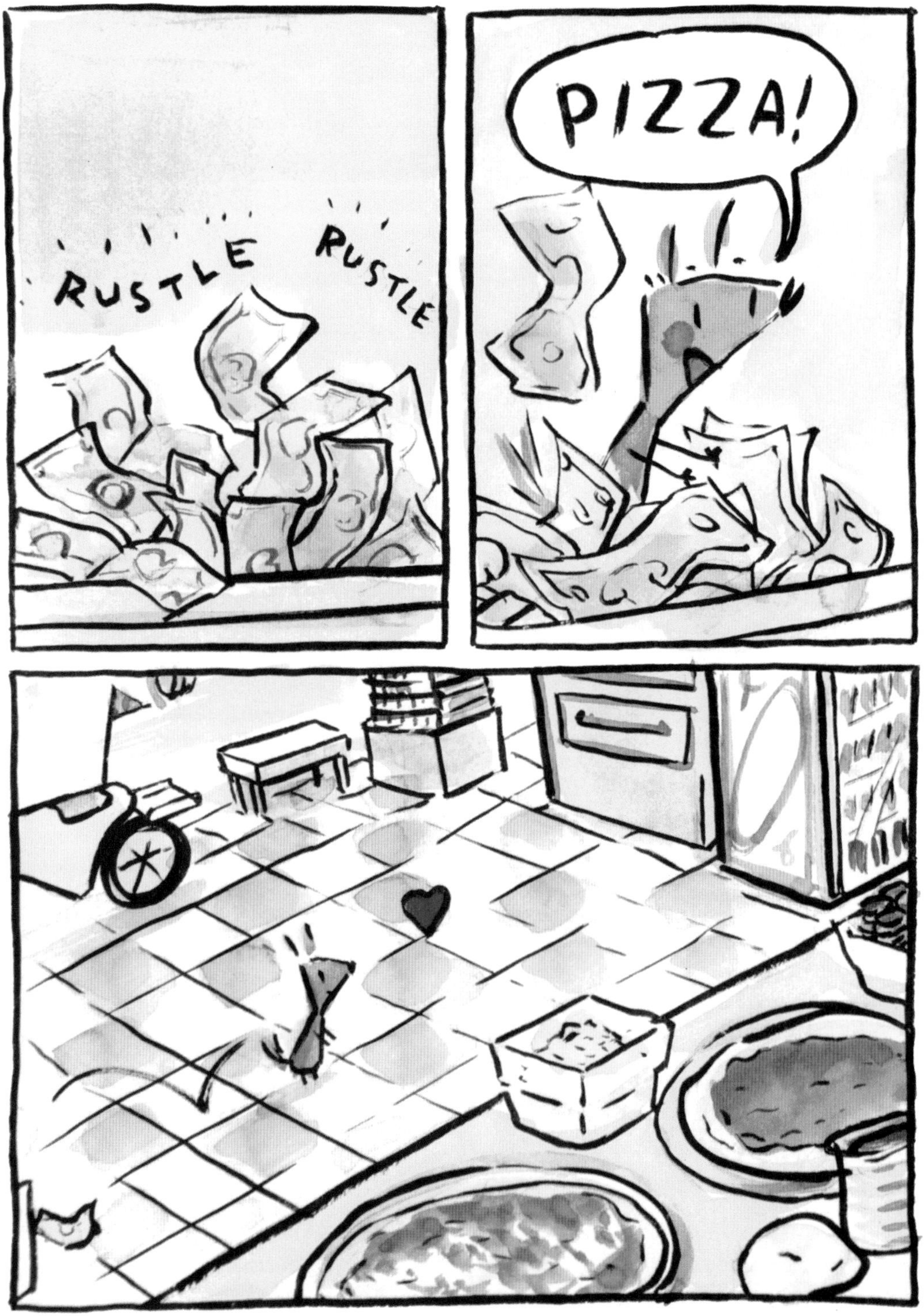
RUSTLE
RUSTLE
PIZZA!

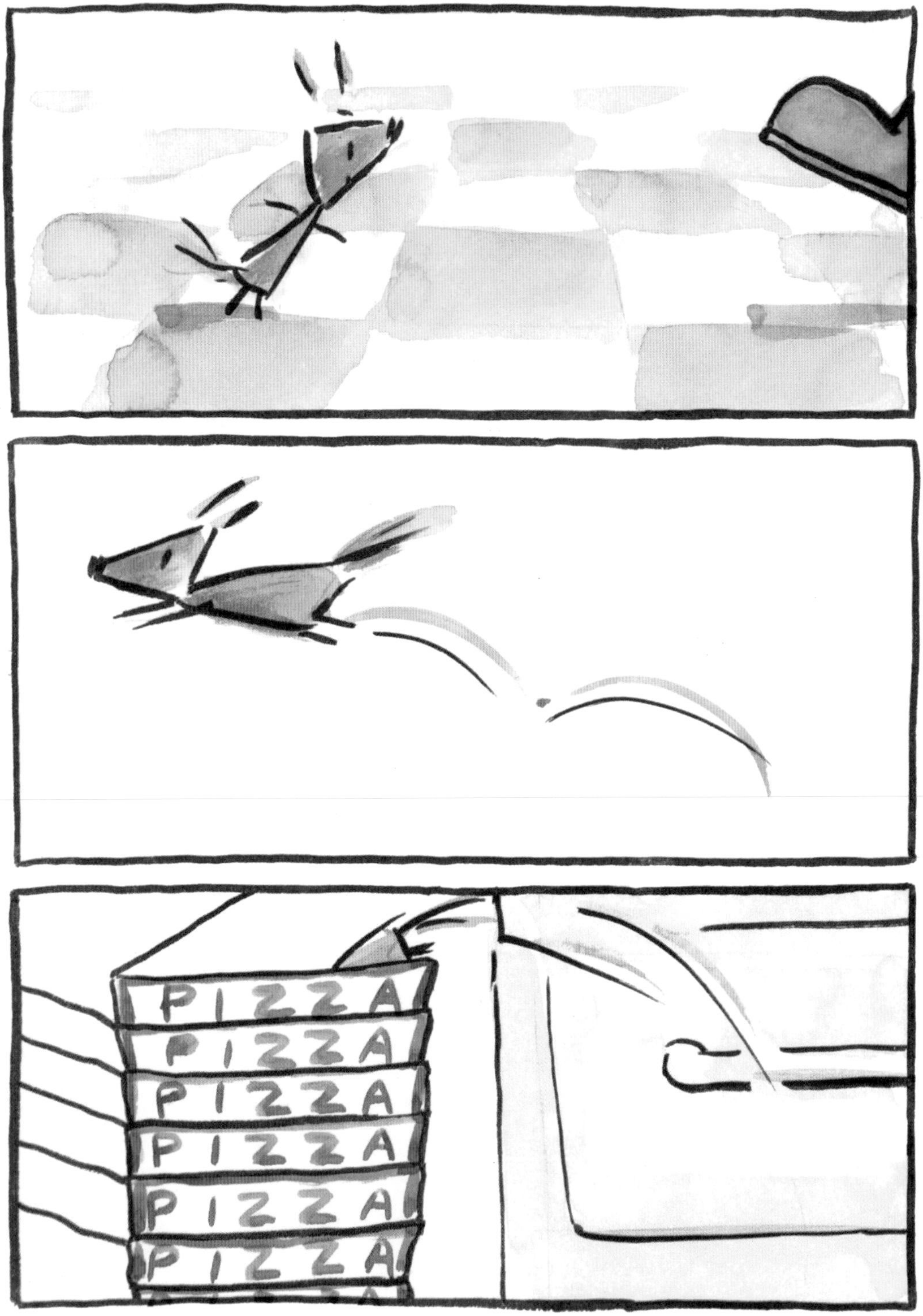
PIZZA
PIZZA
PIZZA
PIZZA
PIZZA
PIZZA

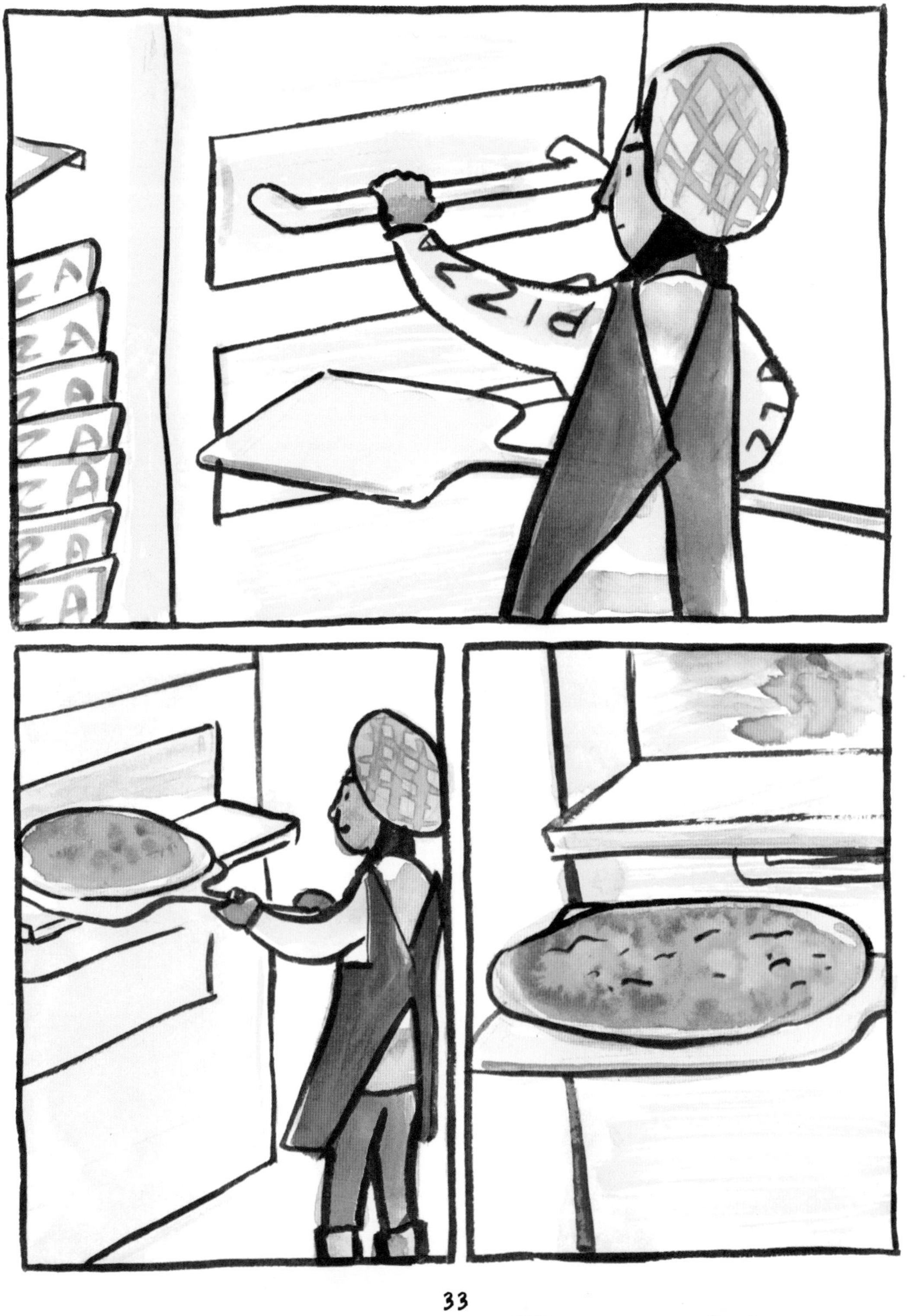

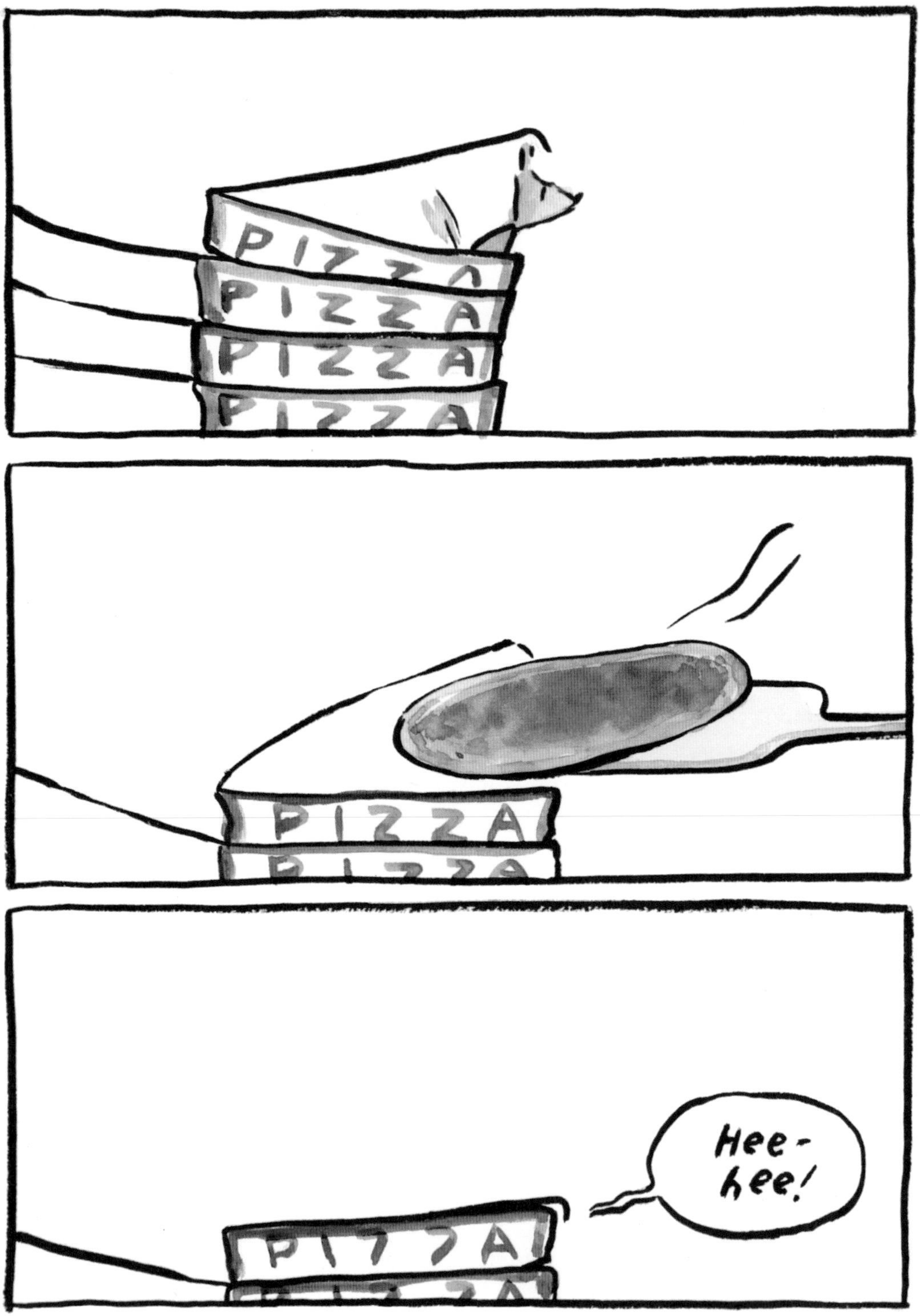
PIZZA
PIZZA
PIZZA
PIZZA
PIZZA
PIZZA
Hee-hee!

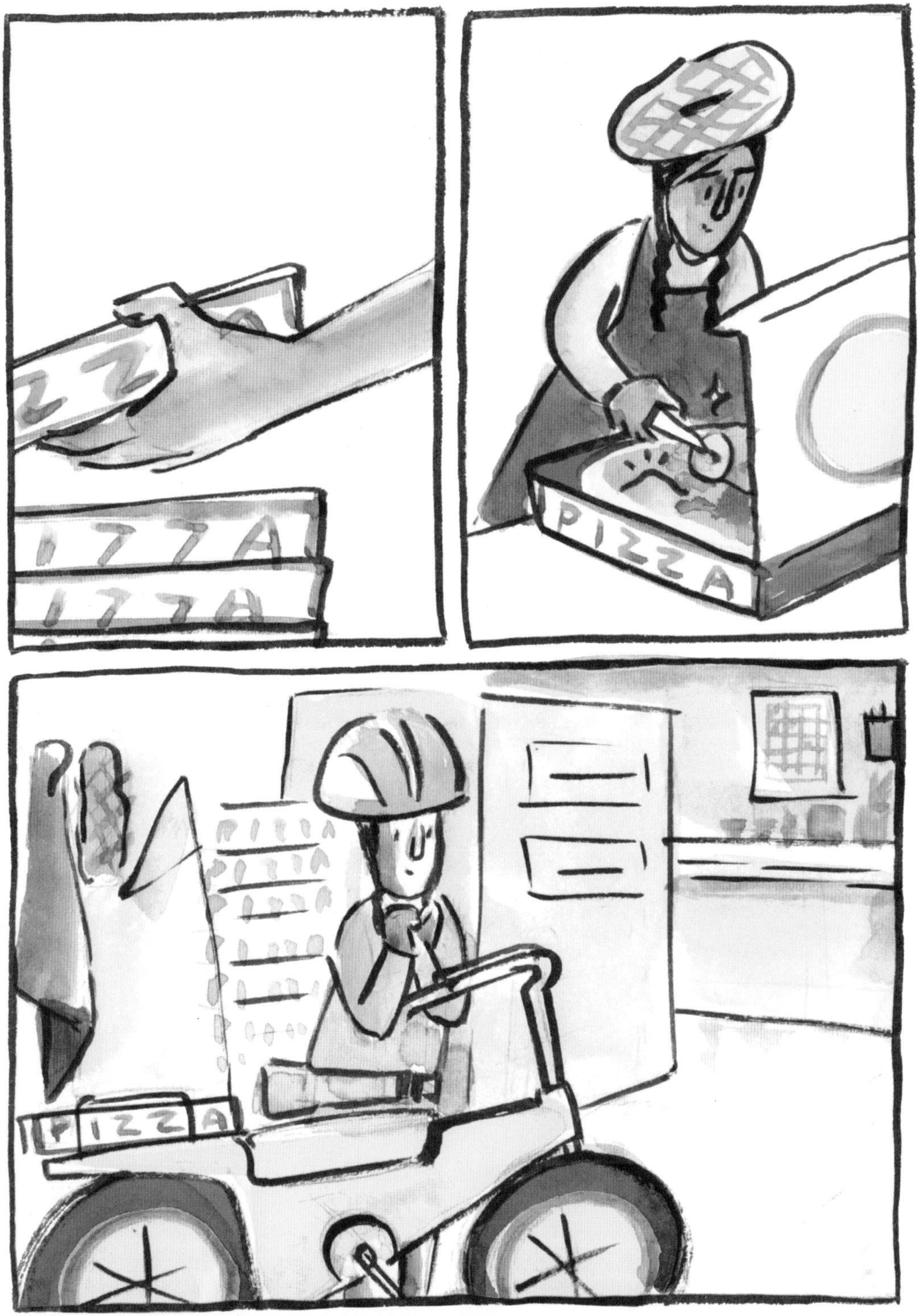
PIZZA
PIZZA

Chapter 4

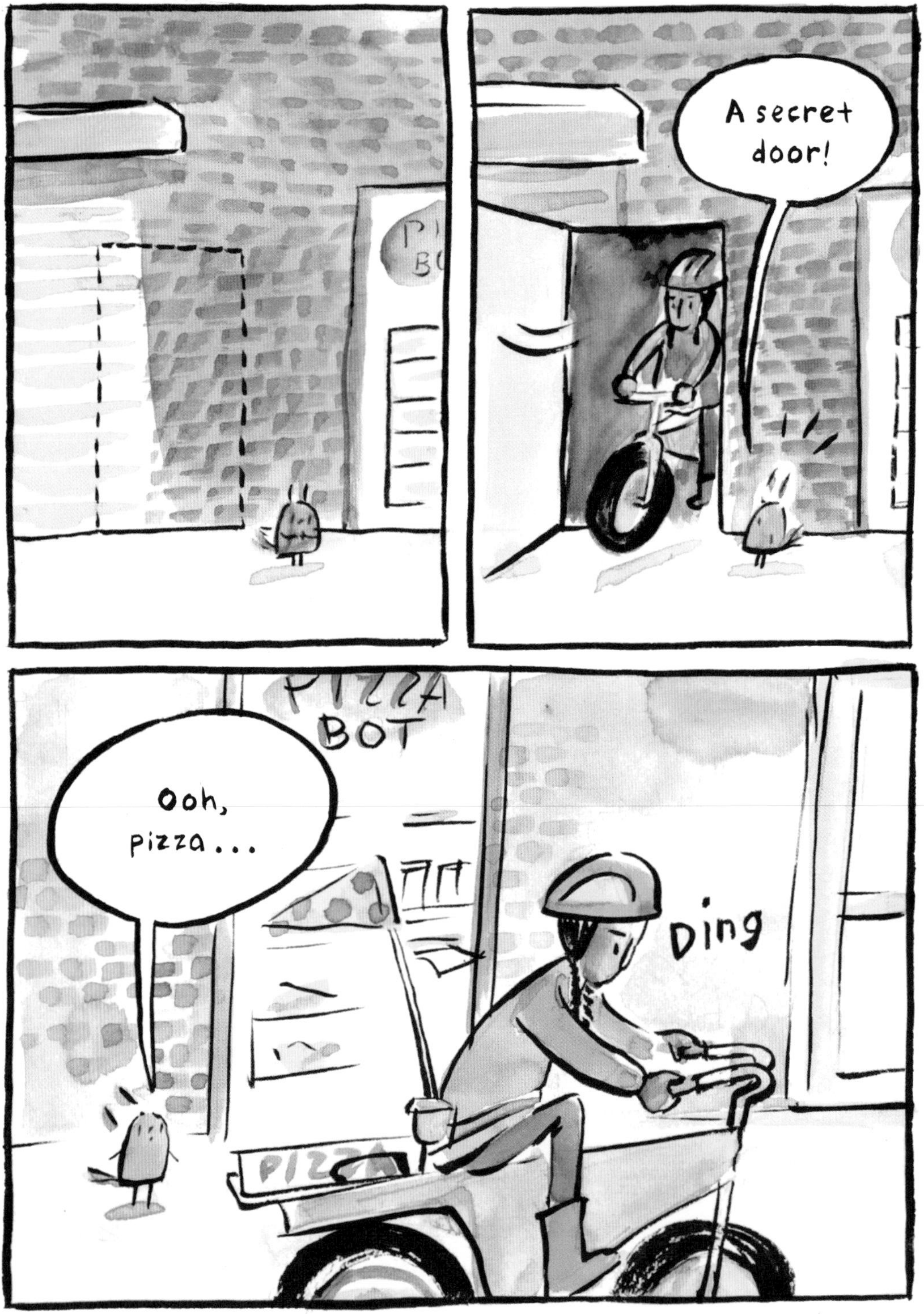

PI
BO
A secret door!
PIZZA
BOT
Ooh, pizza...
Ding
PIZZA

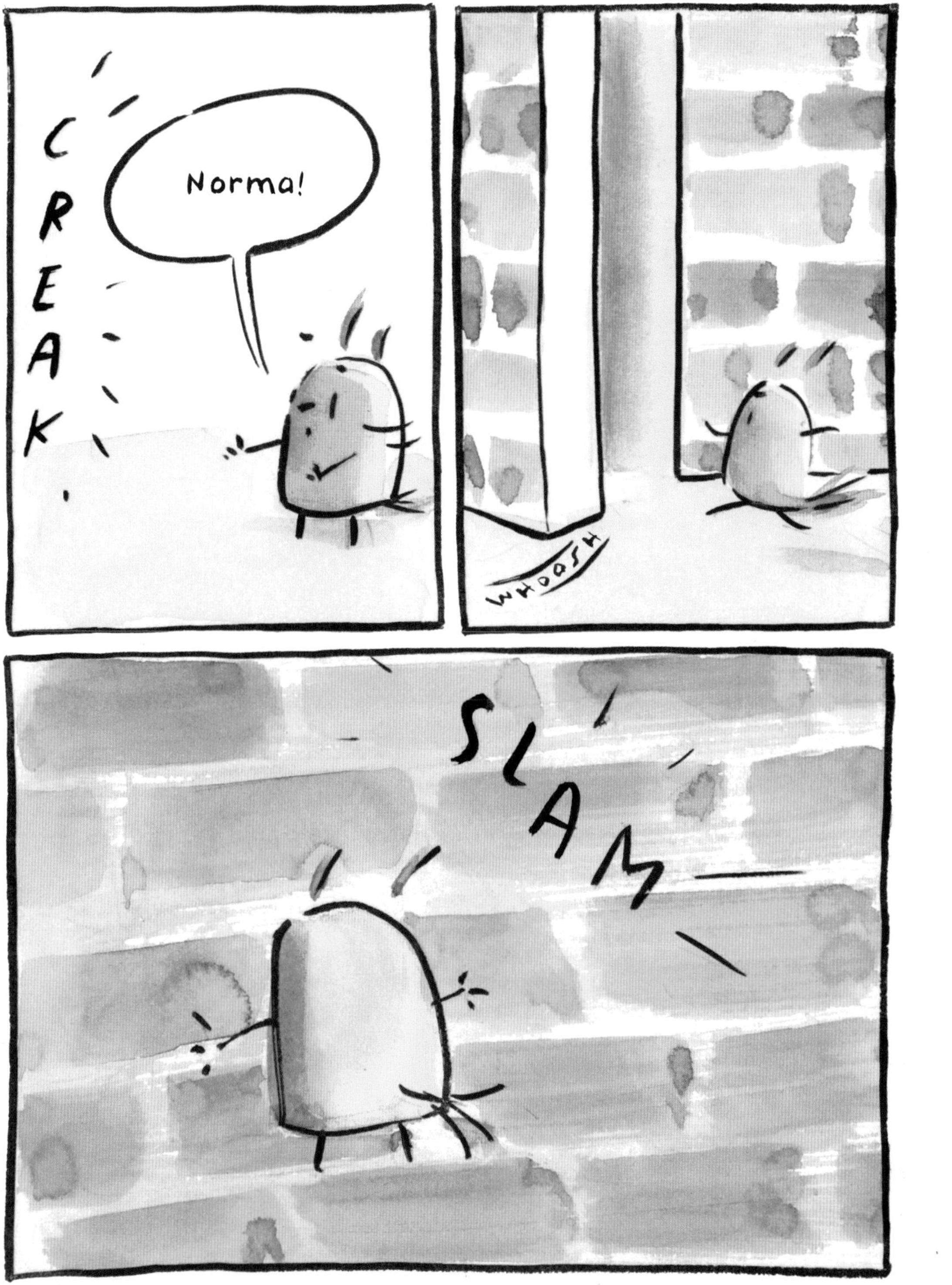
CREAK
Norma!
WHOOSH
SLAM

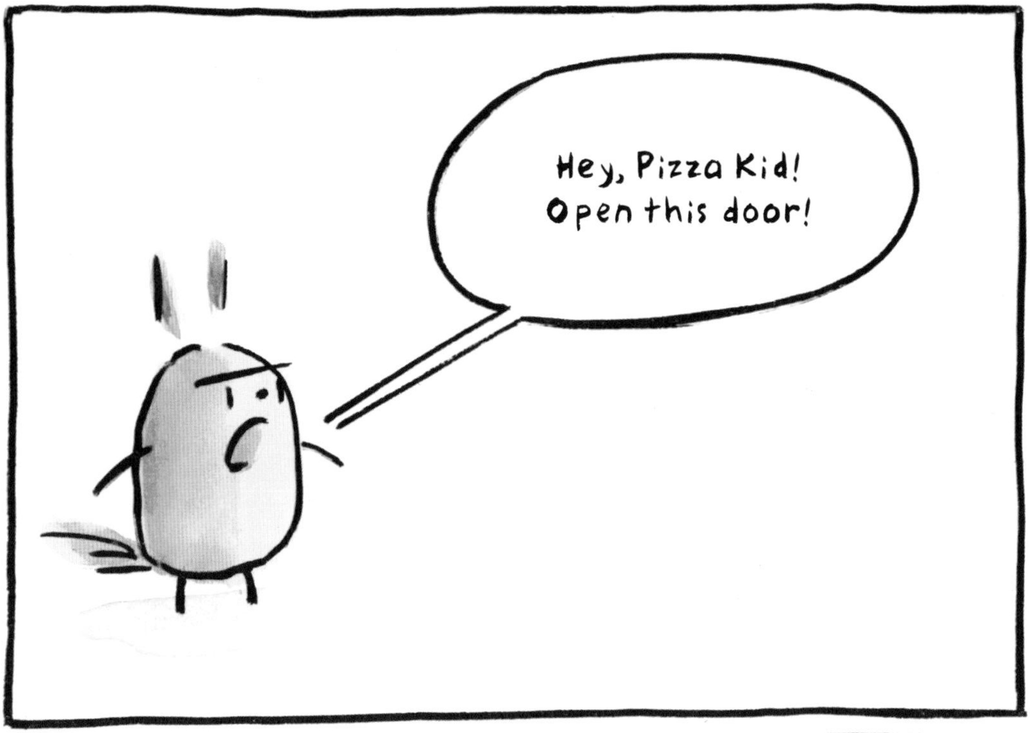
Hey, Pizza Kid!
Open this door!

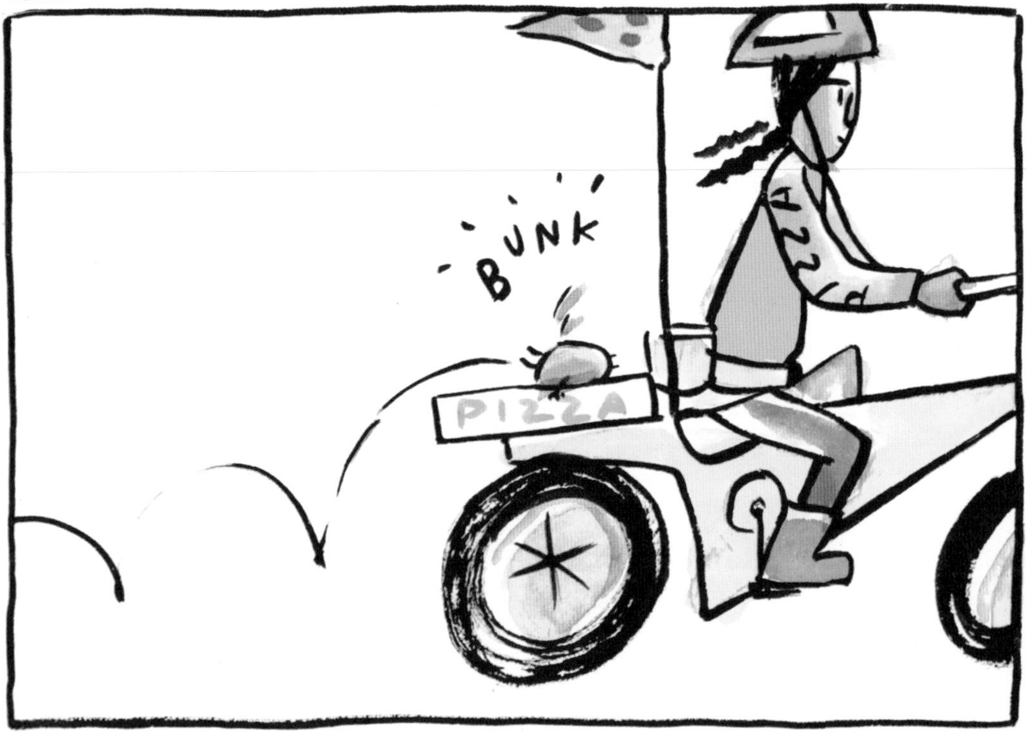
BUNK
PIZZA
PIZZA

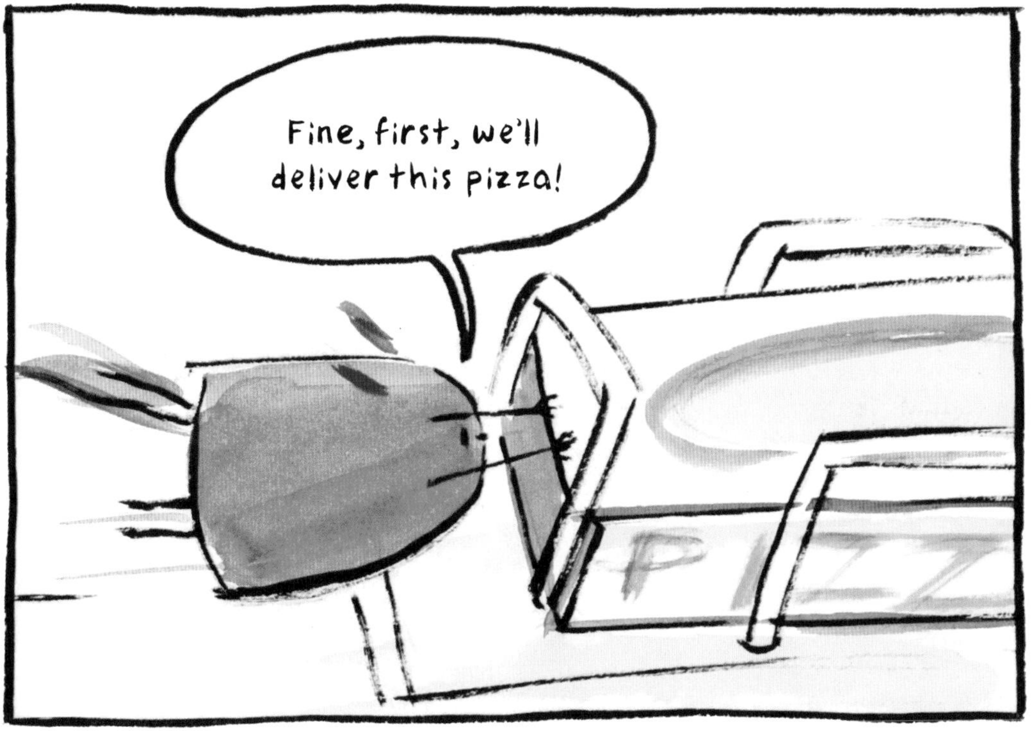
Fine, first, we'll deliver this pizza!

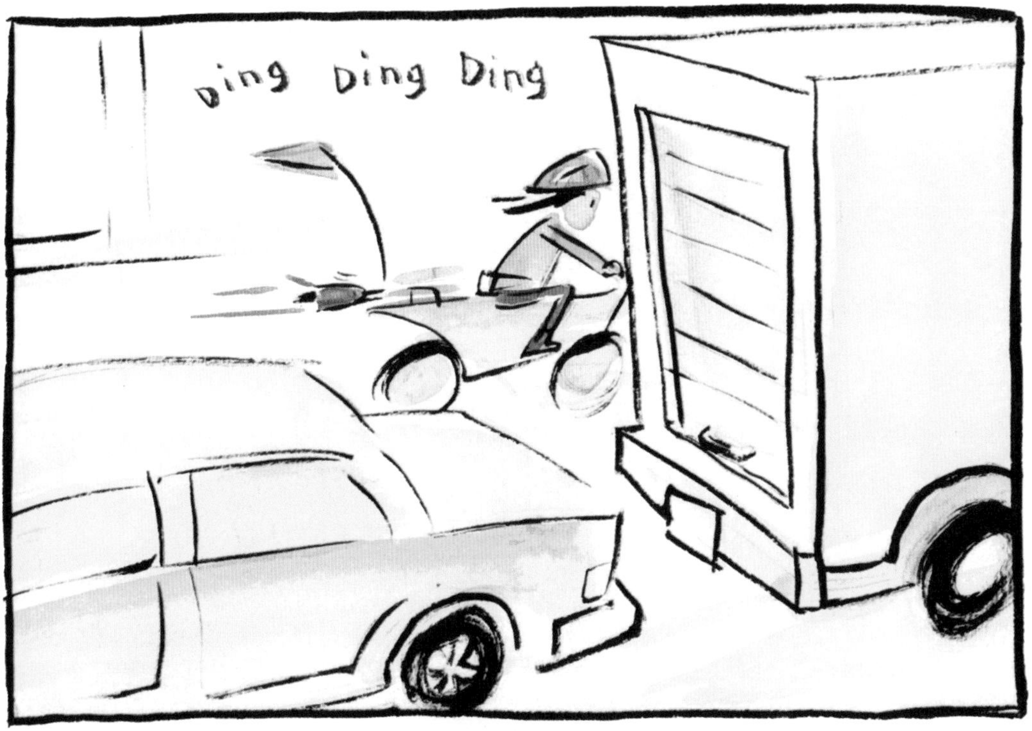
Ding Ding Ding

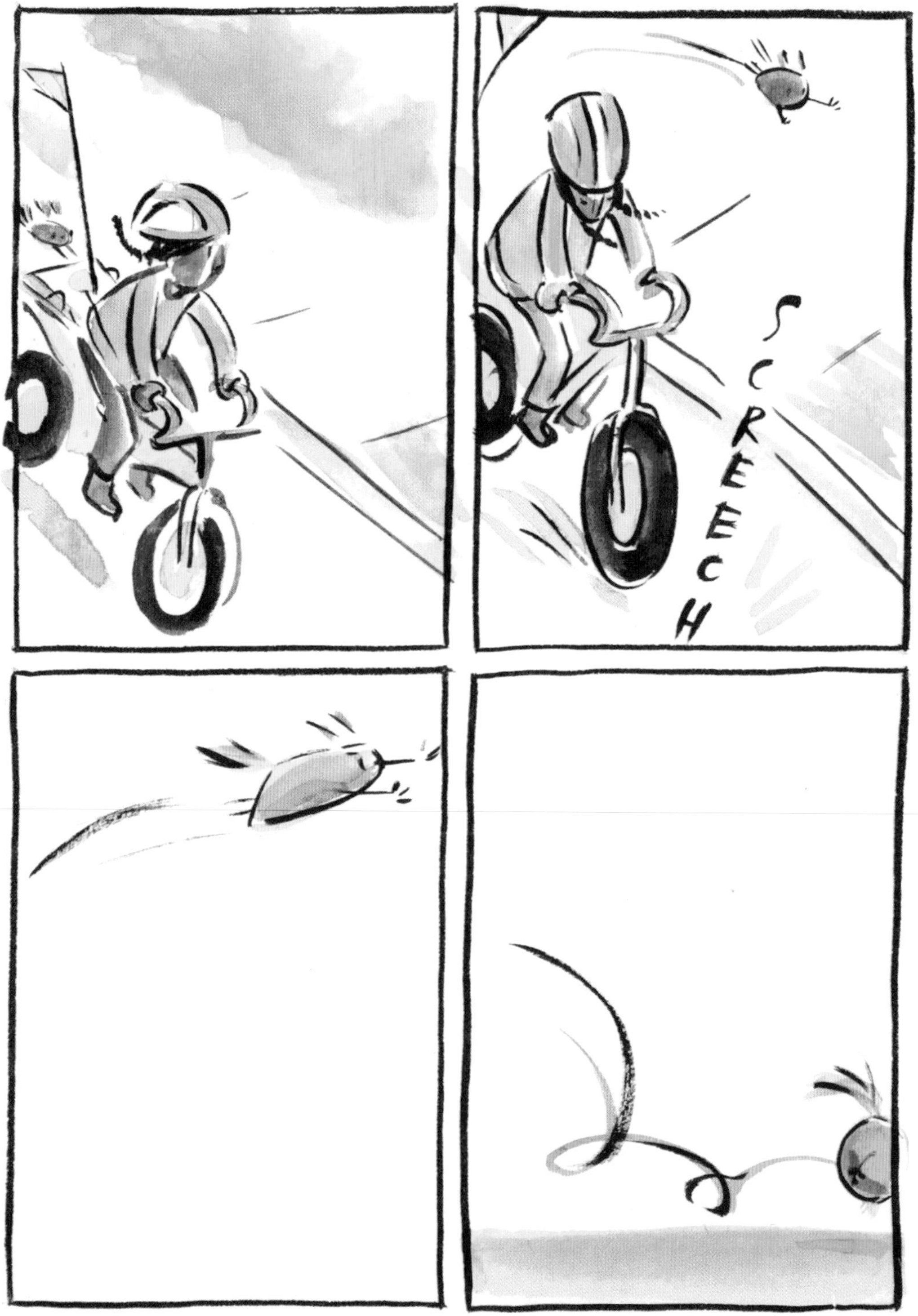
SCREECH

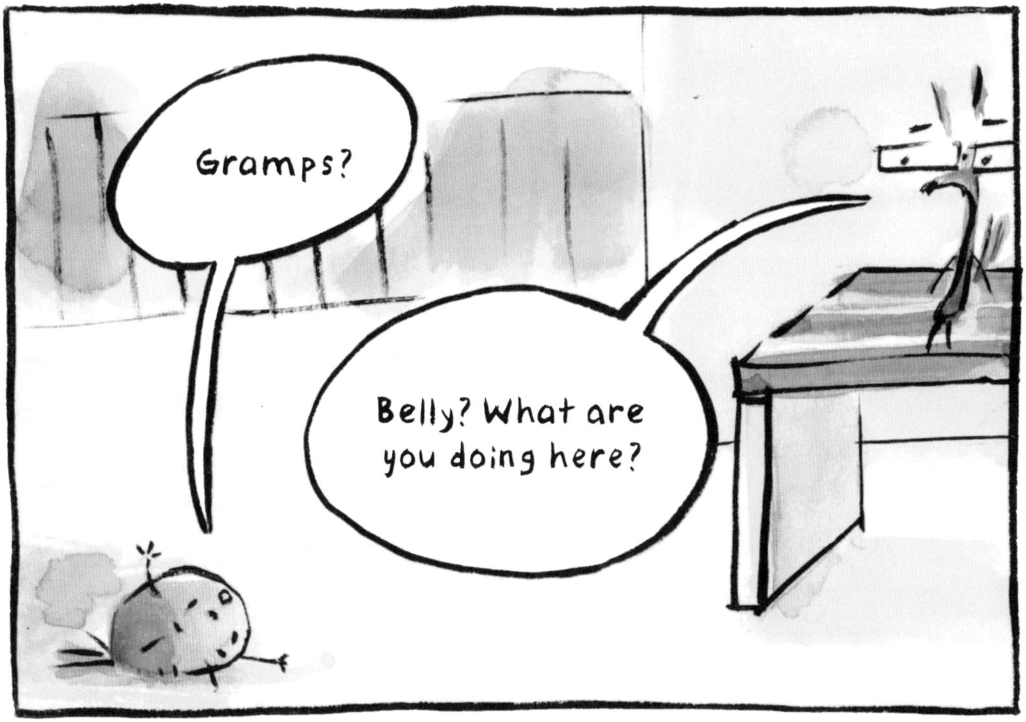
Gramps?
Belly? What are you doing here?

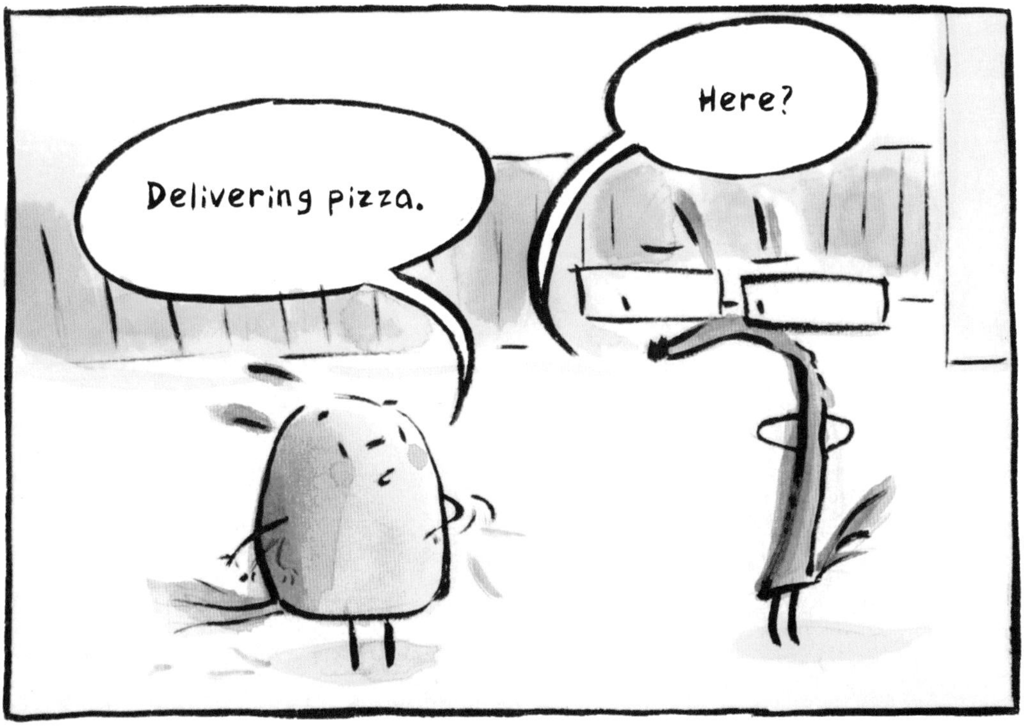
Here?
Delivering pizza.

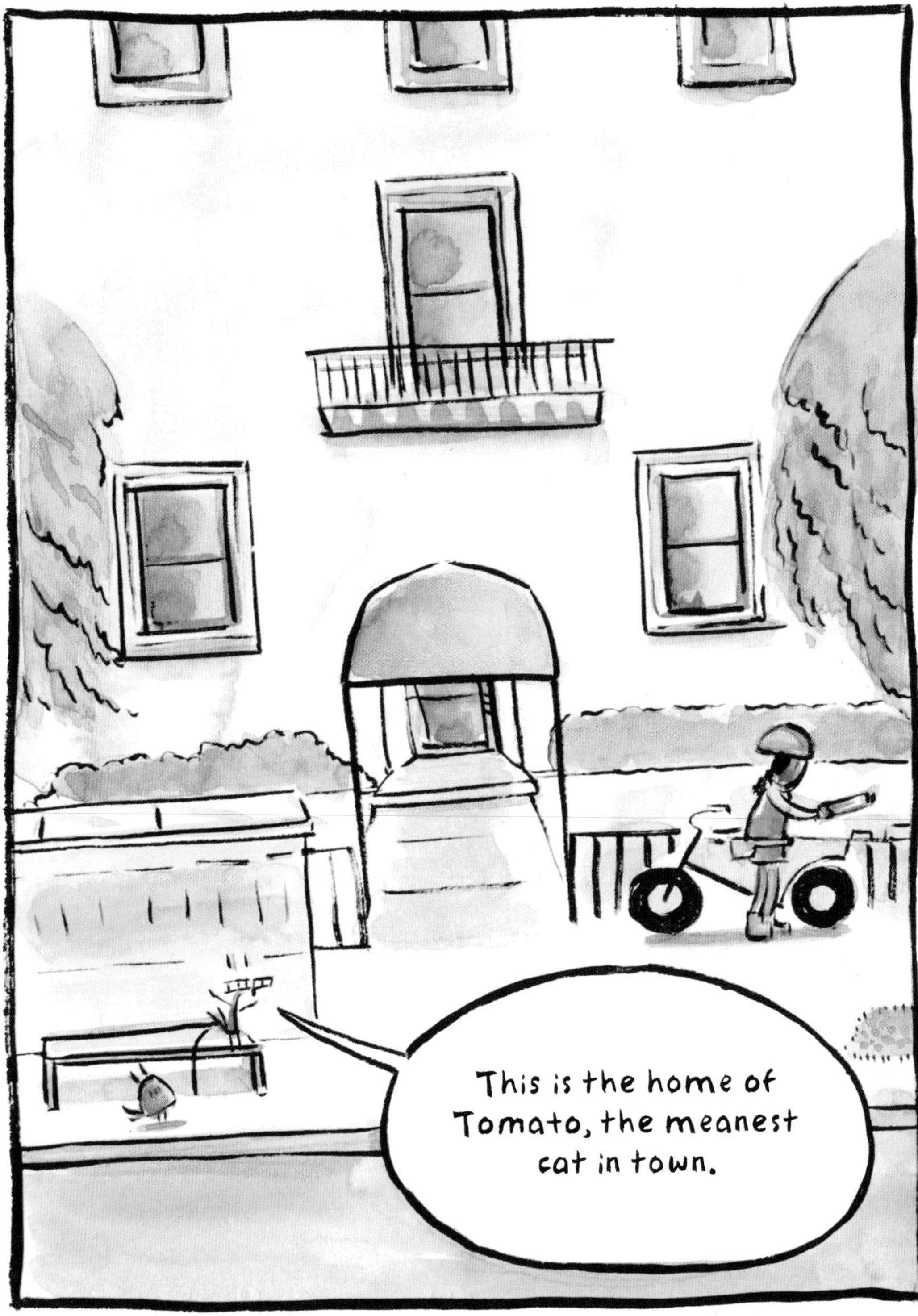
This is the home of Tomato, the meanest cat in town.

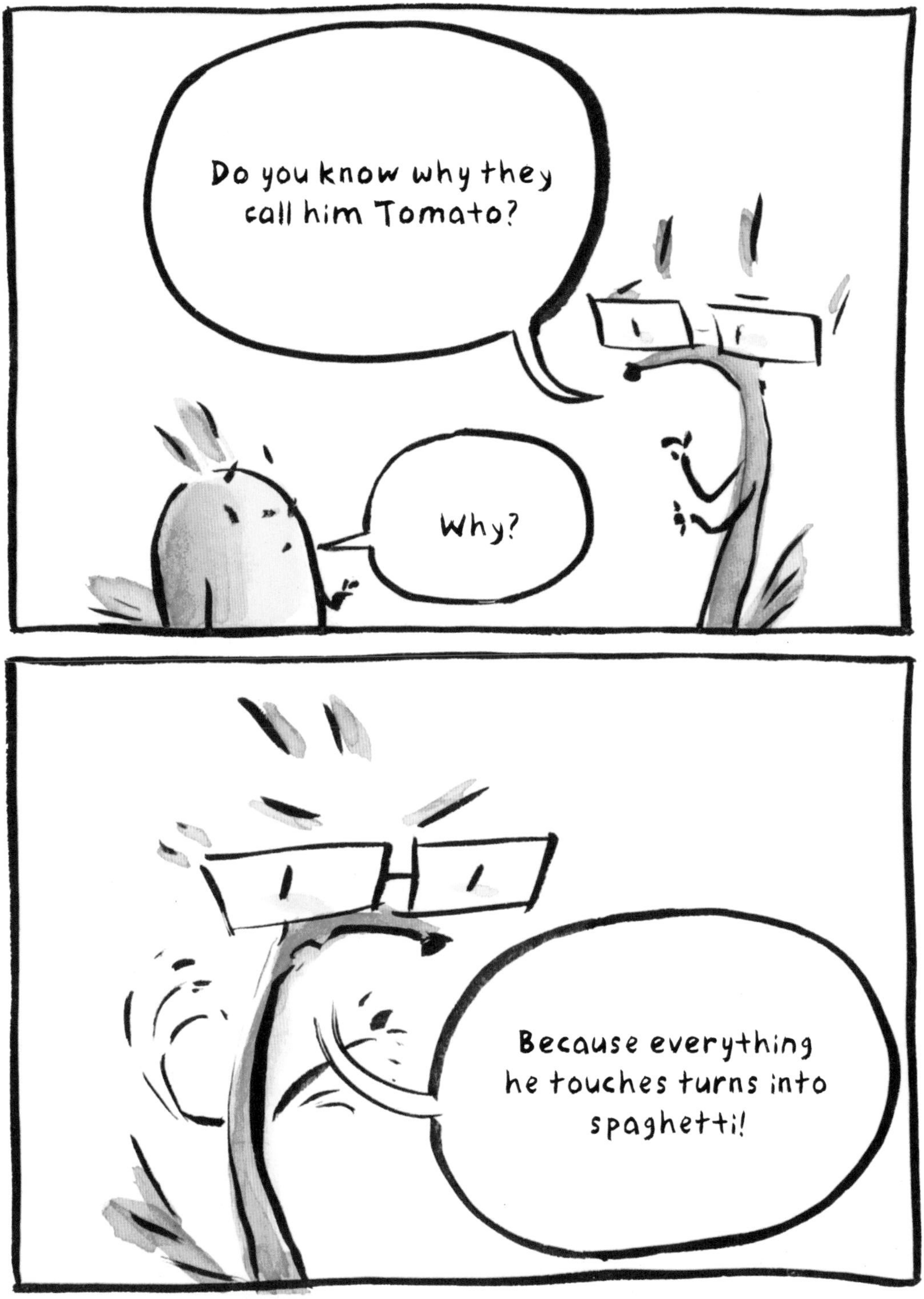

Do you know why they call him Tomato?
Why?
Because everything he touches turns into spaghetti!

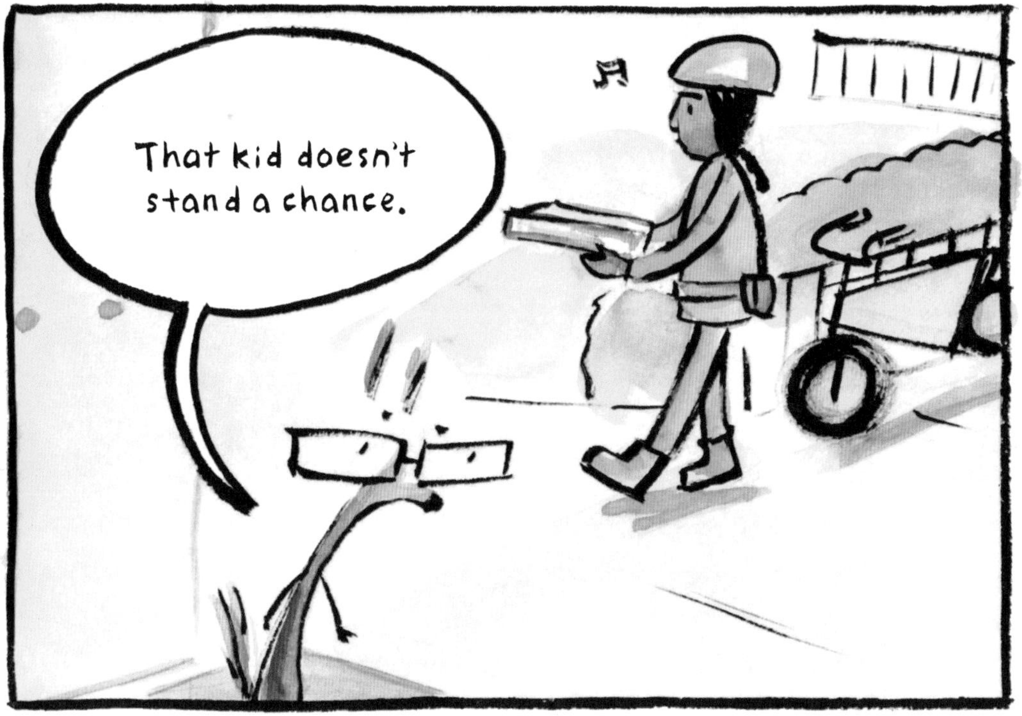
That kid doesn't stand a chance.

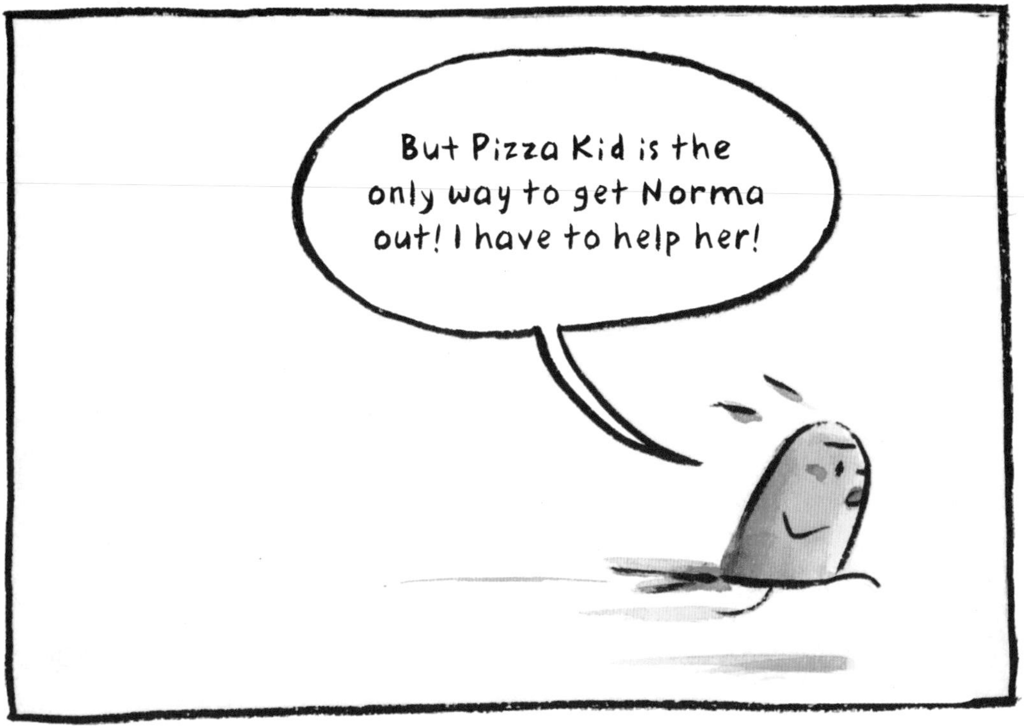
But Pizza Kid is the only way to get Norma out! I have to help her!

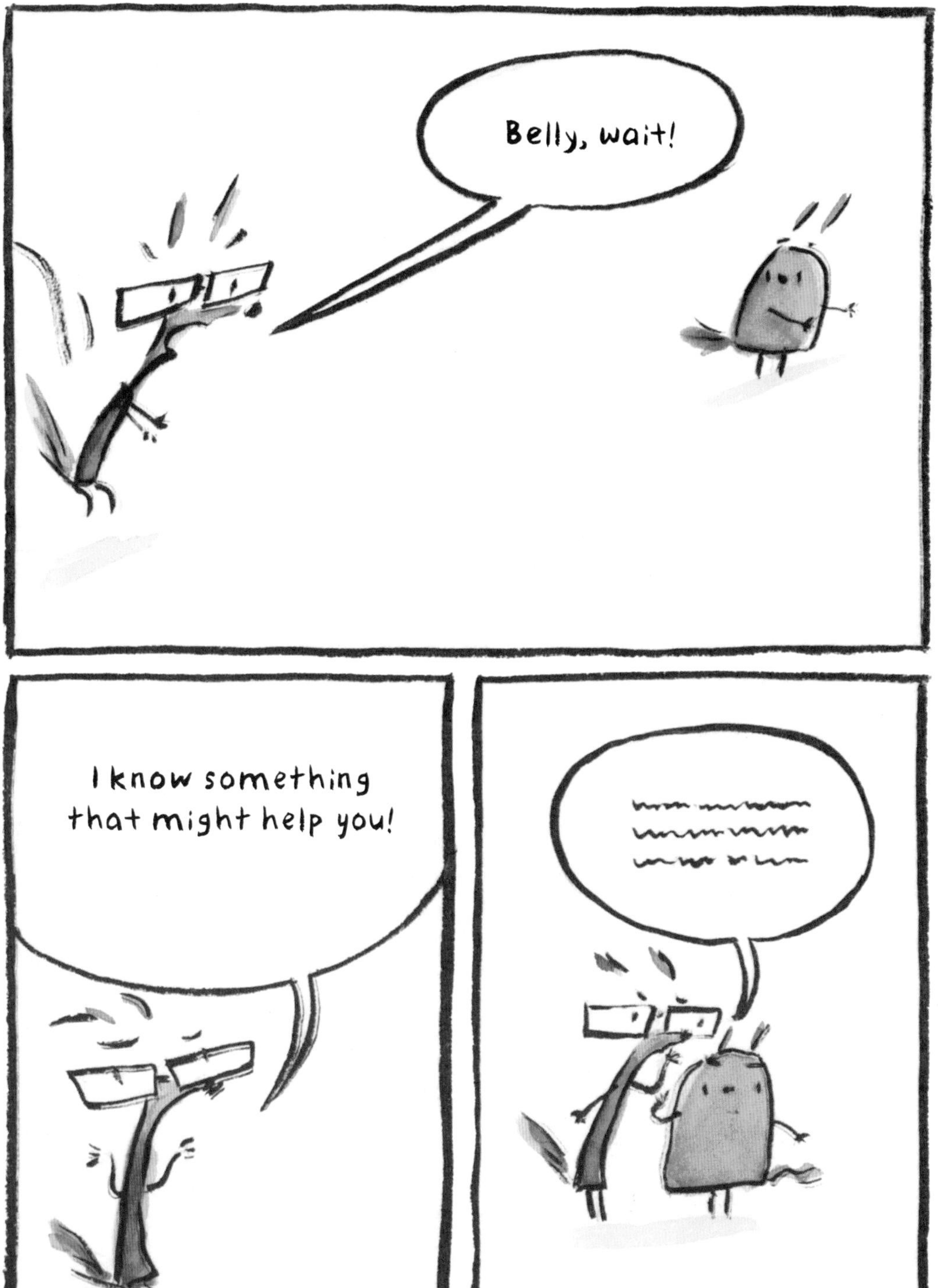
Belly, wait!
I know something that might help you!

Chapter 5

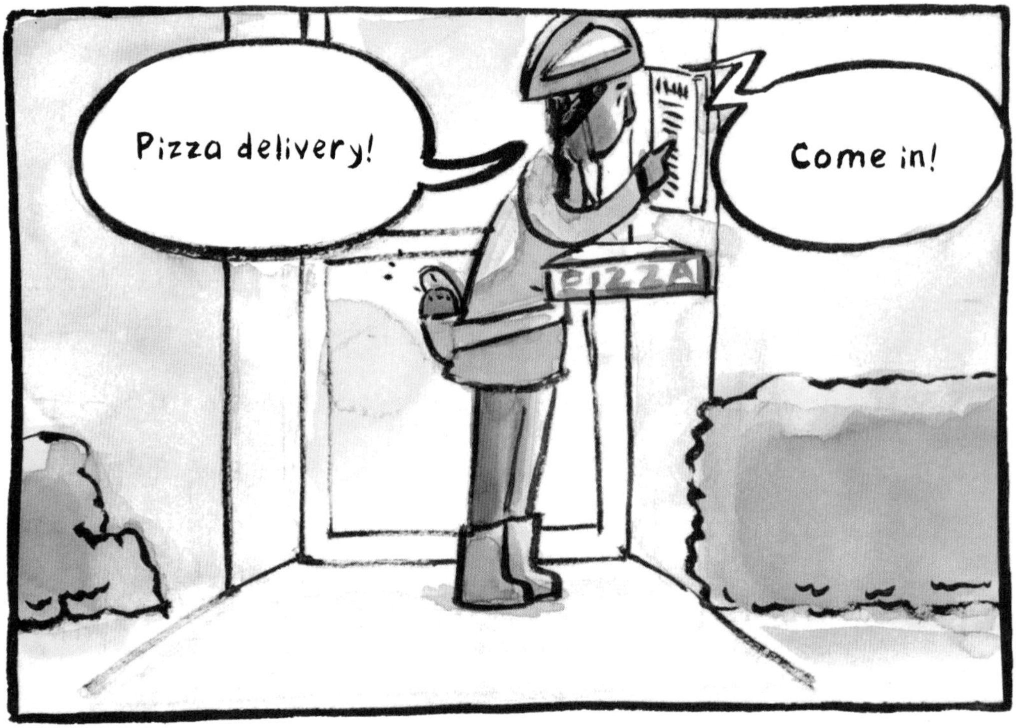
Pizza delivery!
Come in!
PIZZA

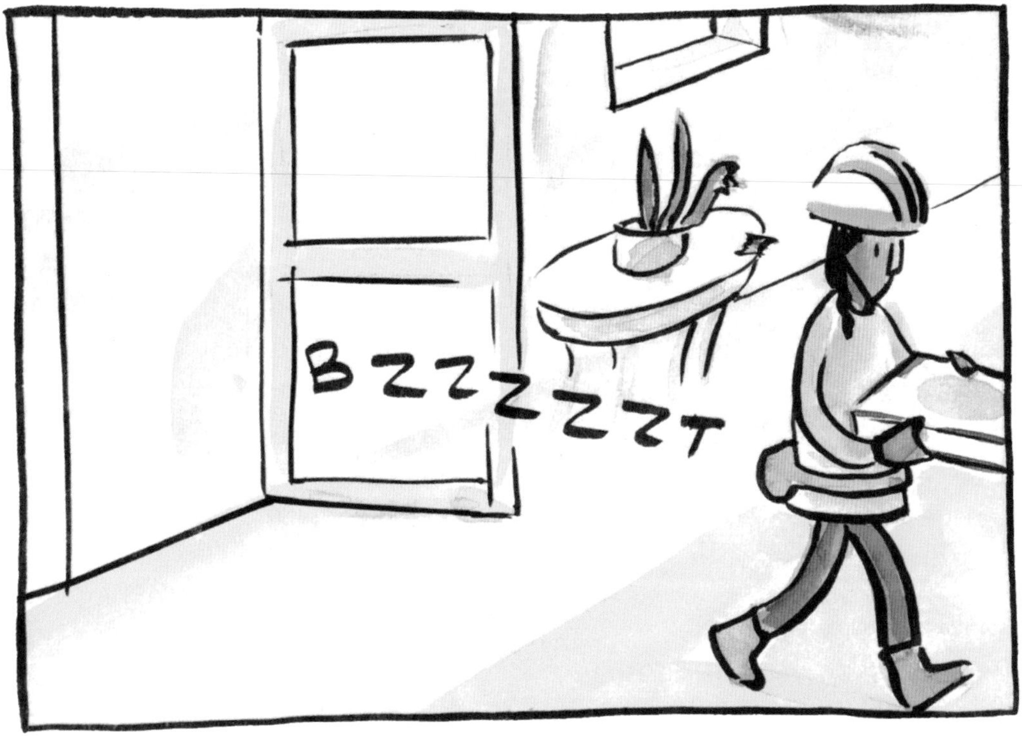
BZZZZZZT

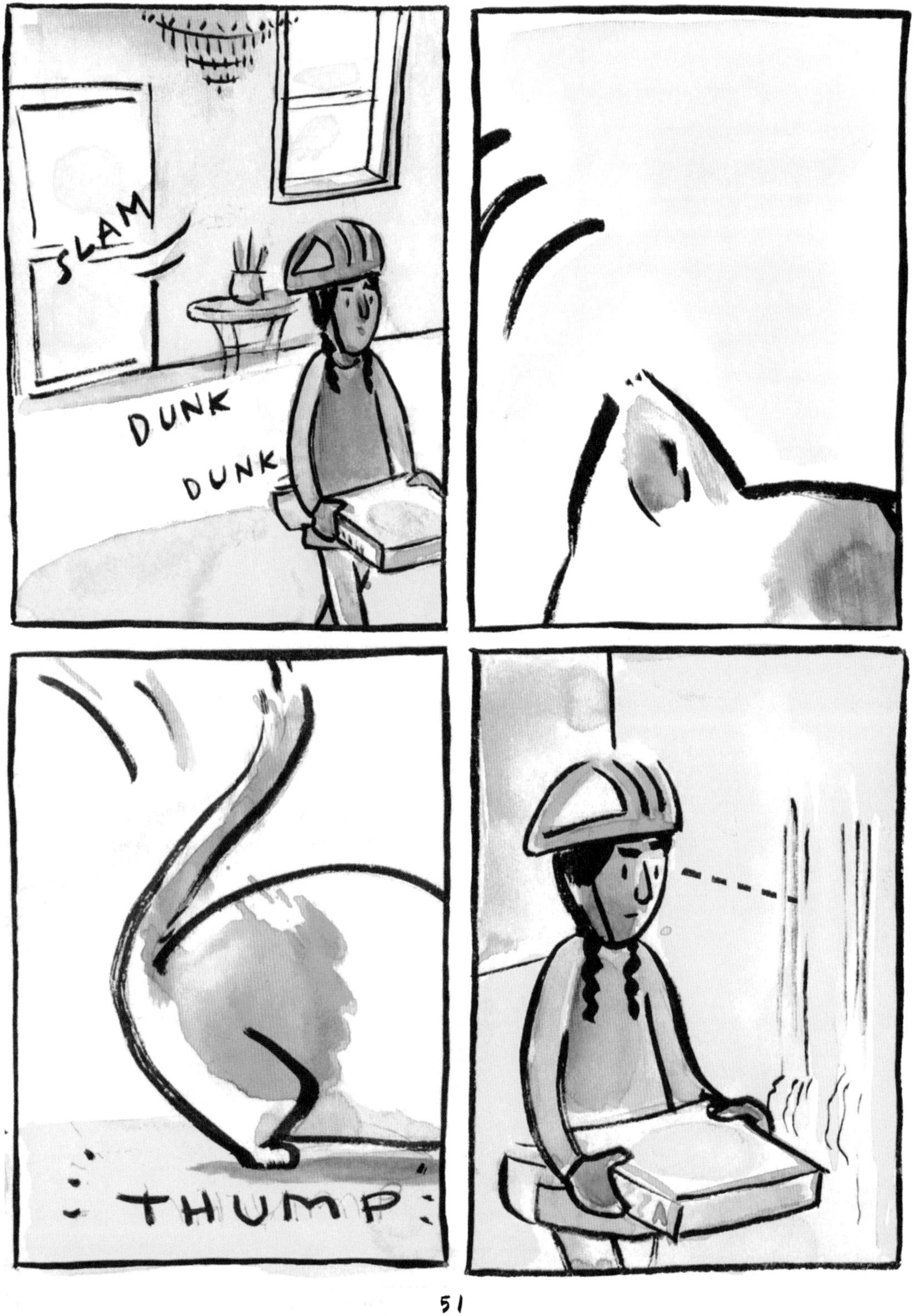
SLAM
DUNK
DUNK
THUMP

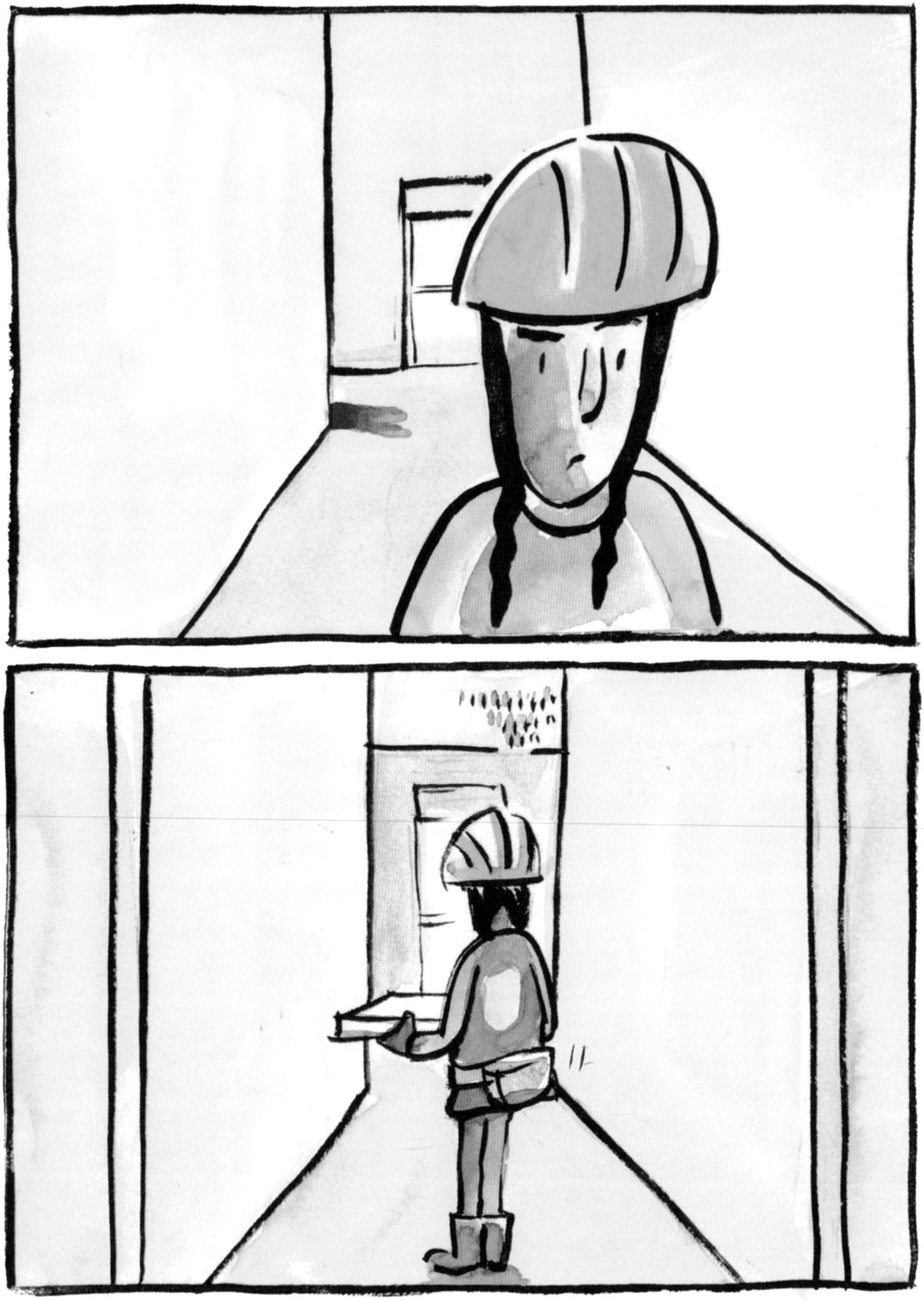

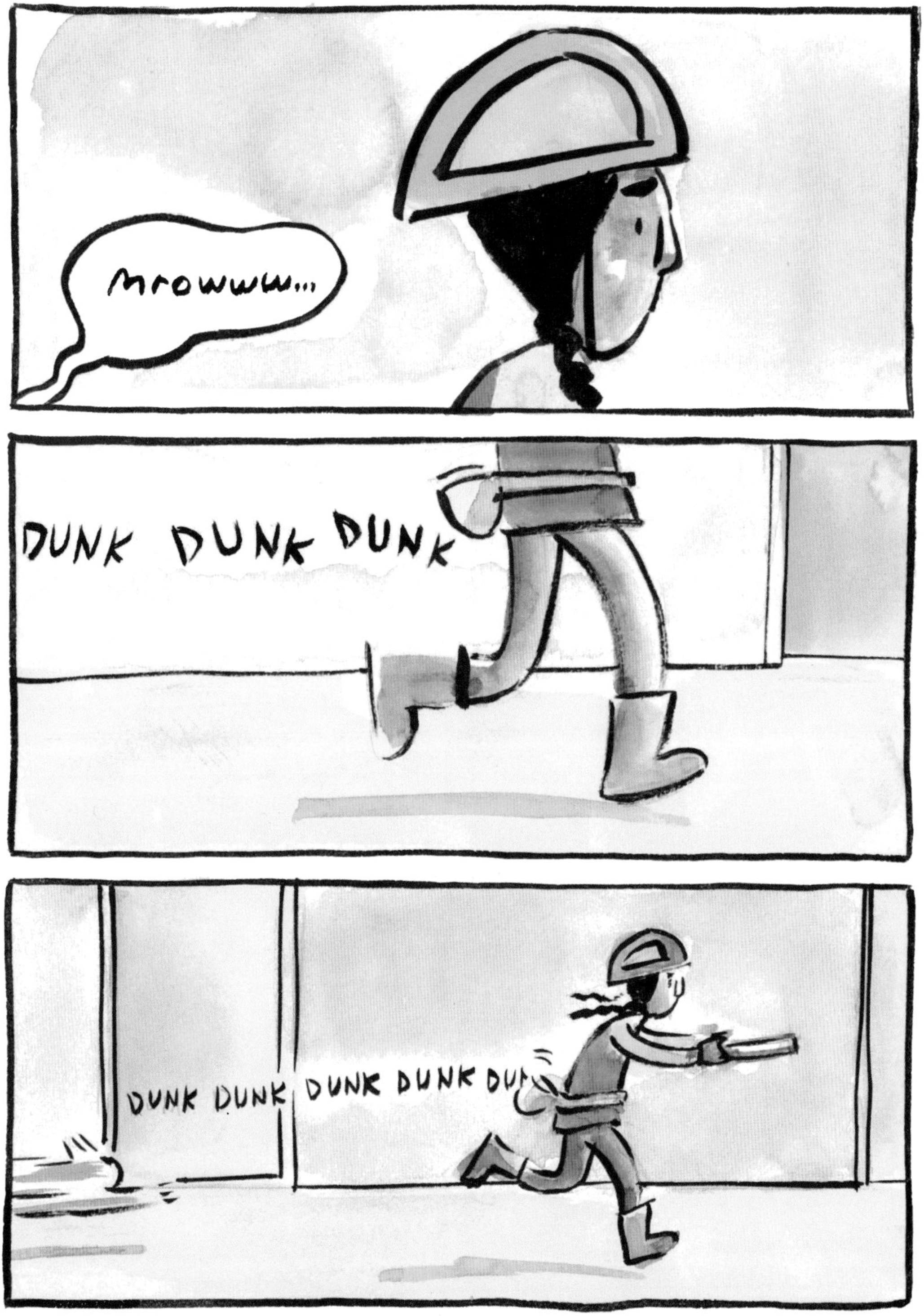
mrowww...
DUNK DUNK DUNK
DUNK DUNK DUNK DUNK DU

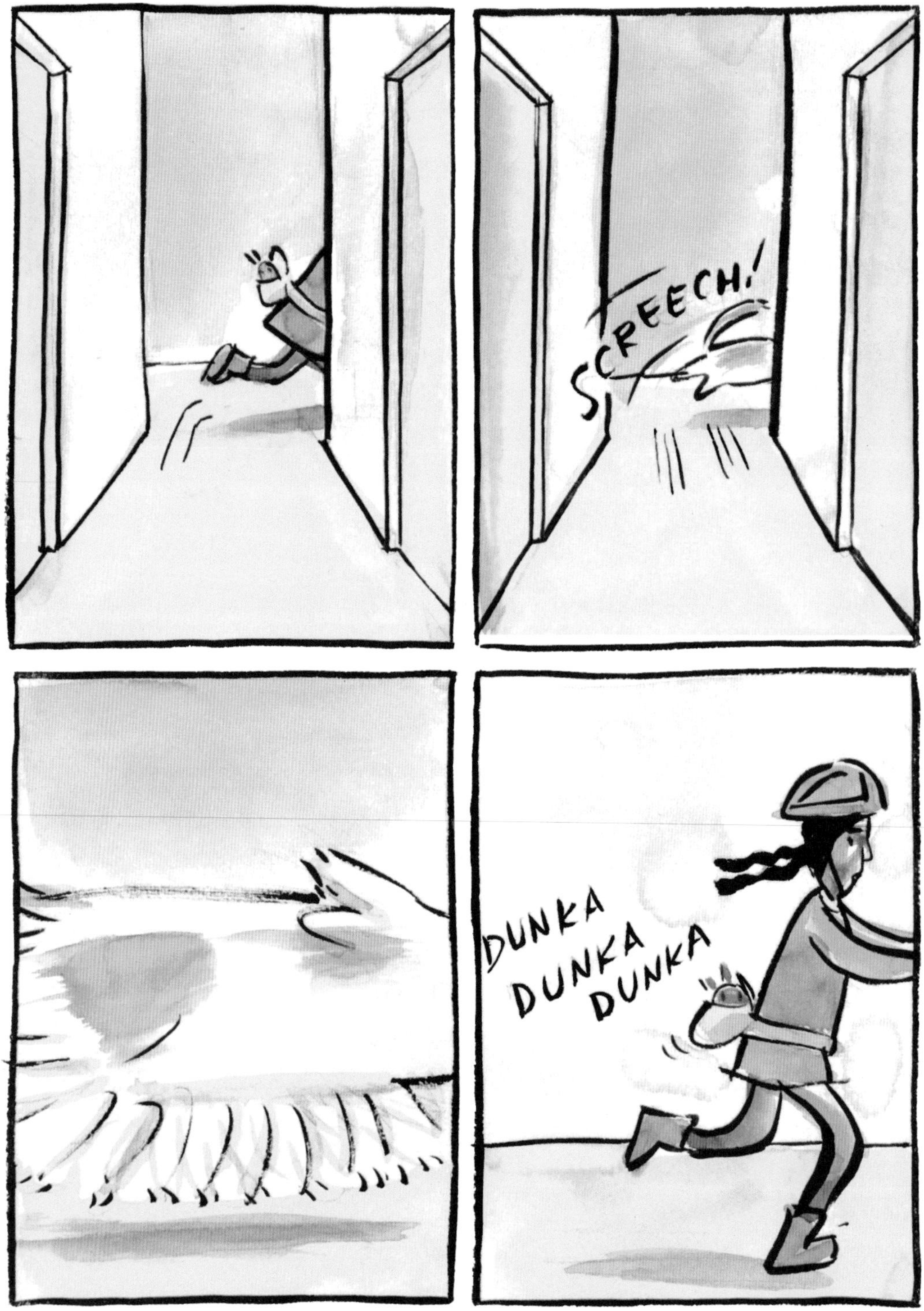
SCREECH!
DUNKA
DUNKA
DUNKA

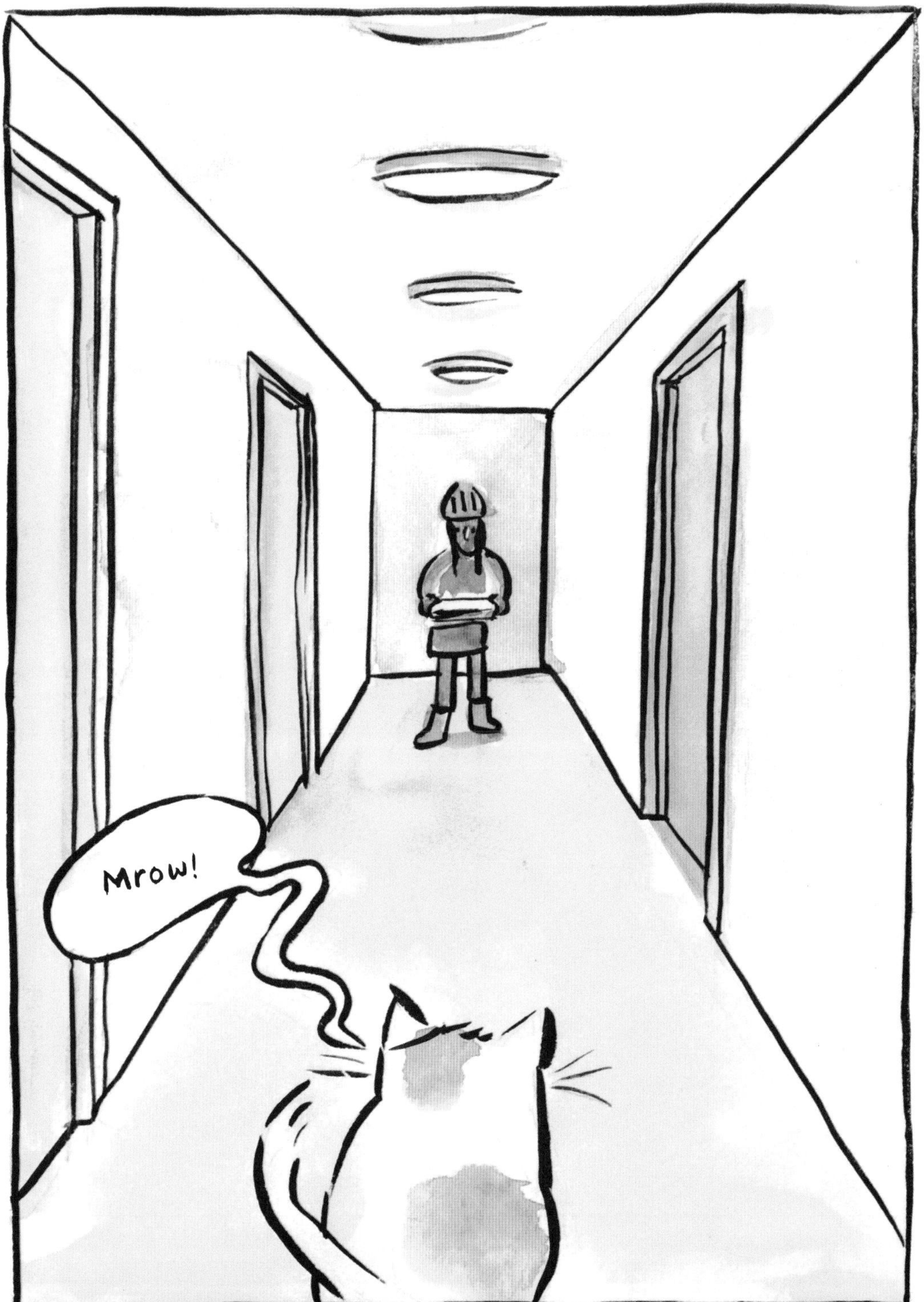
Mrow!

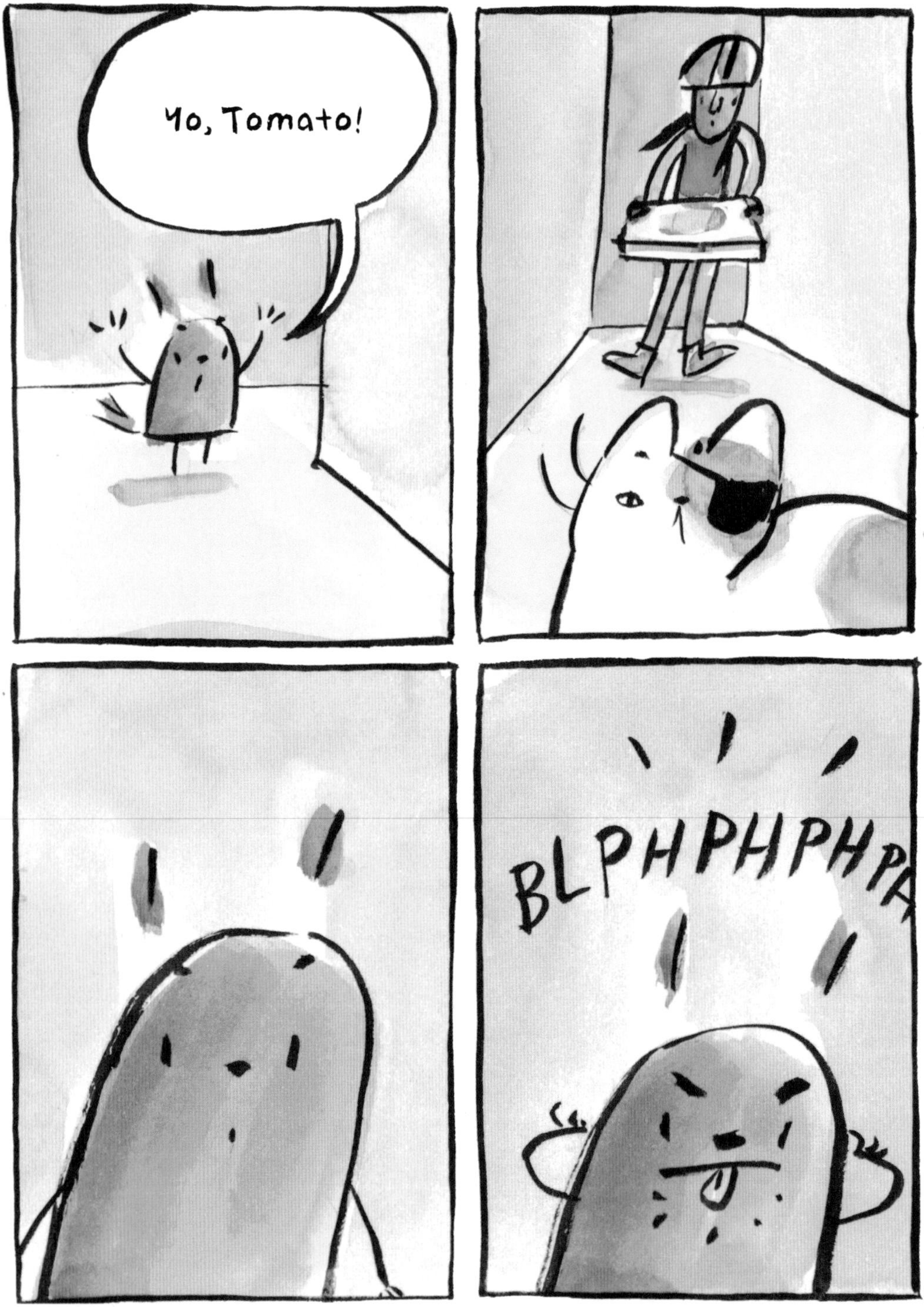

Yo, Tomato!
BLPHPHPHPH

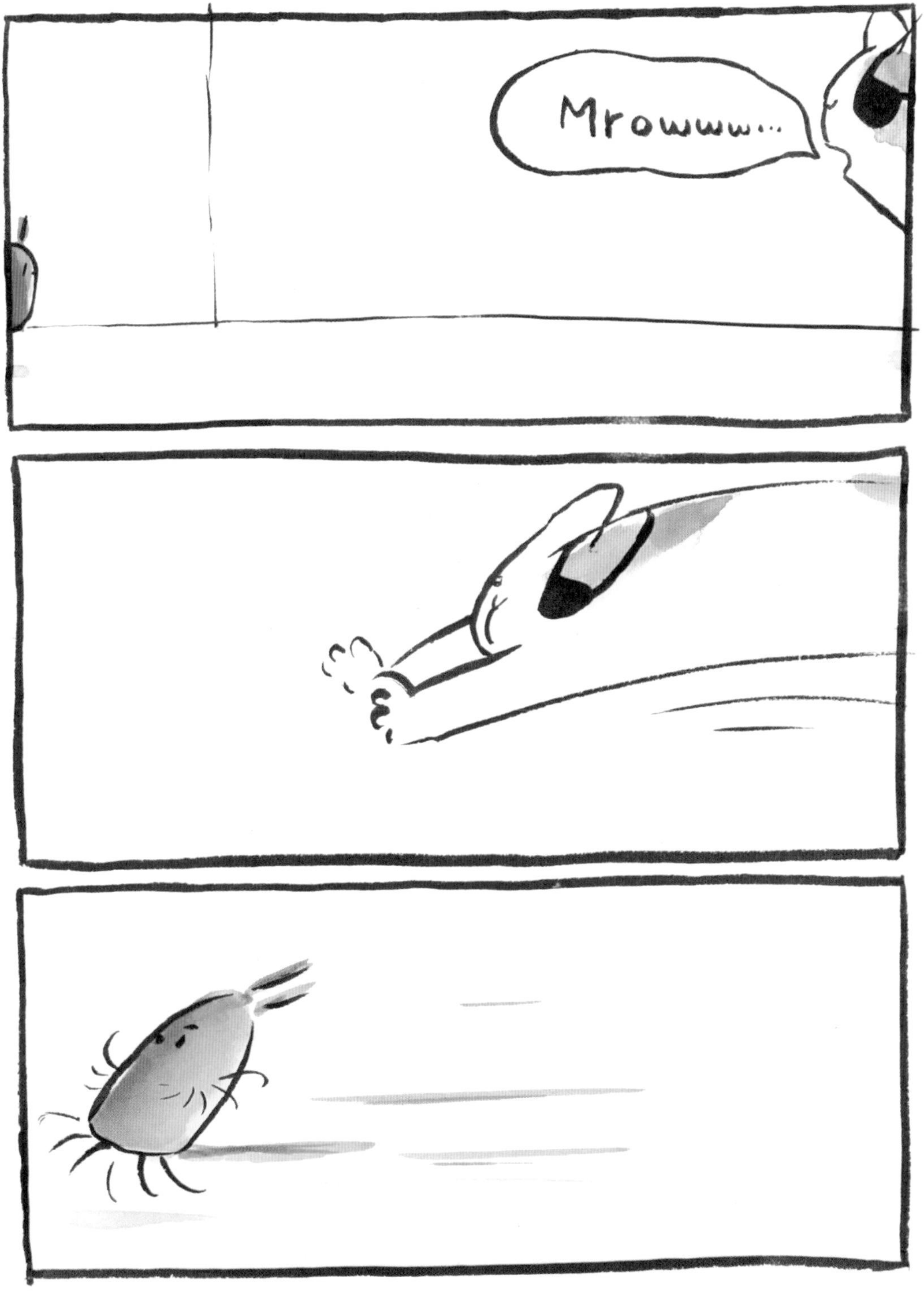
Mrowww...

chapter 6

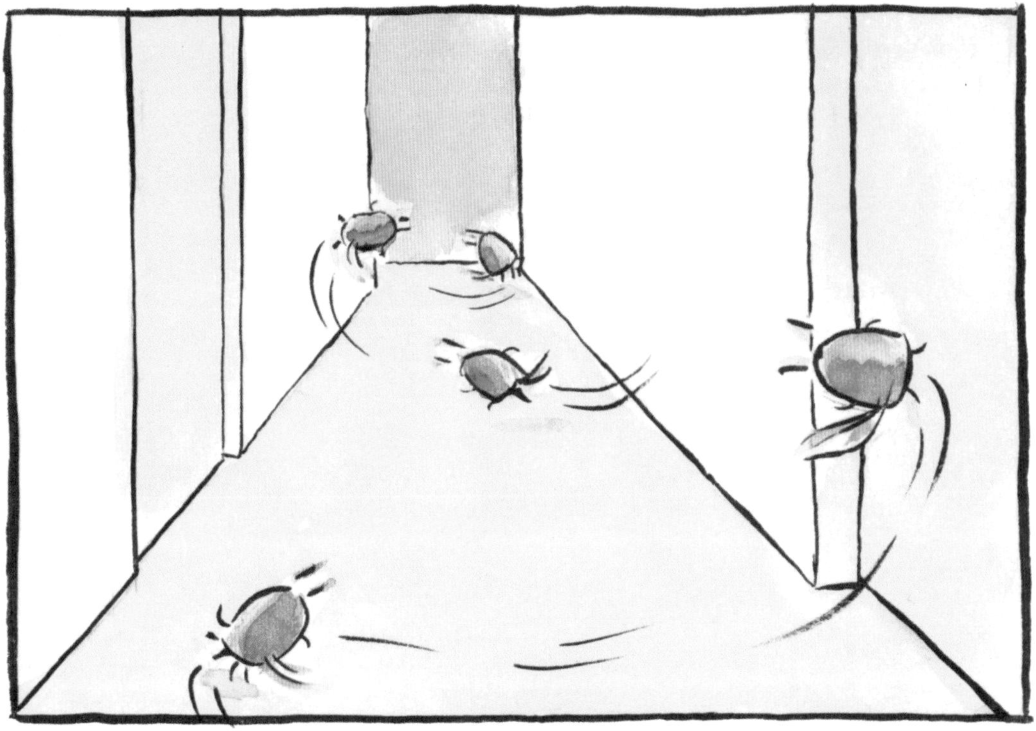

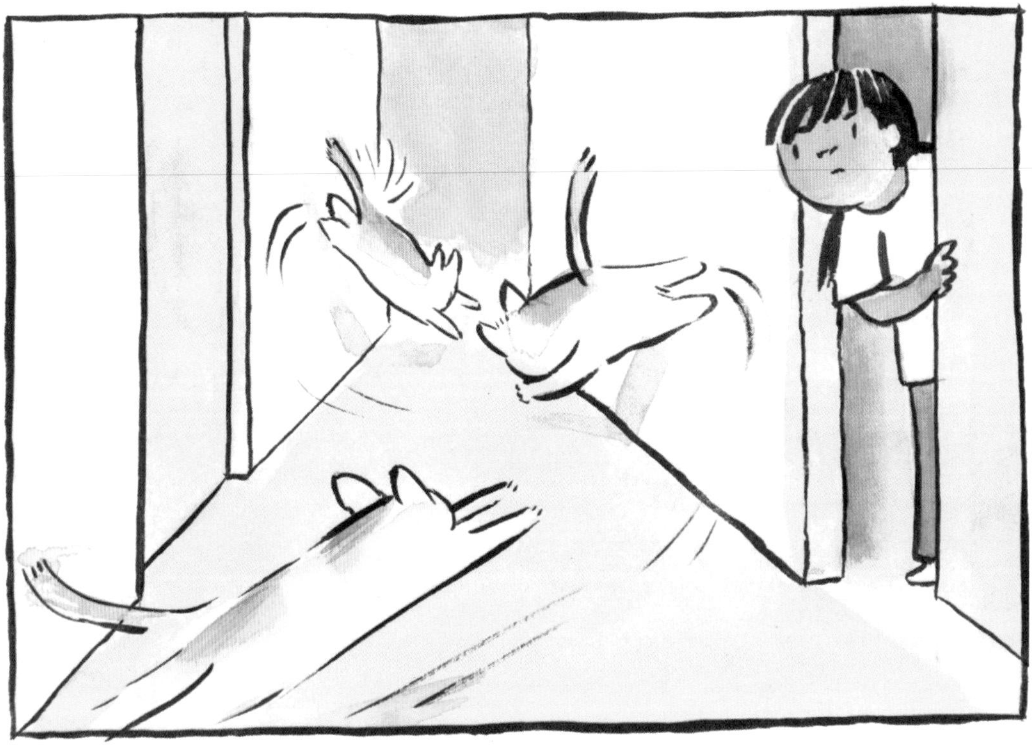

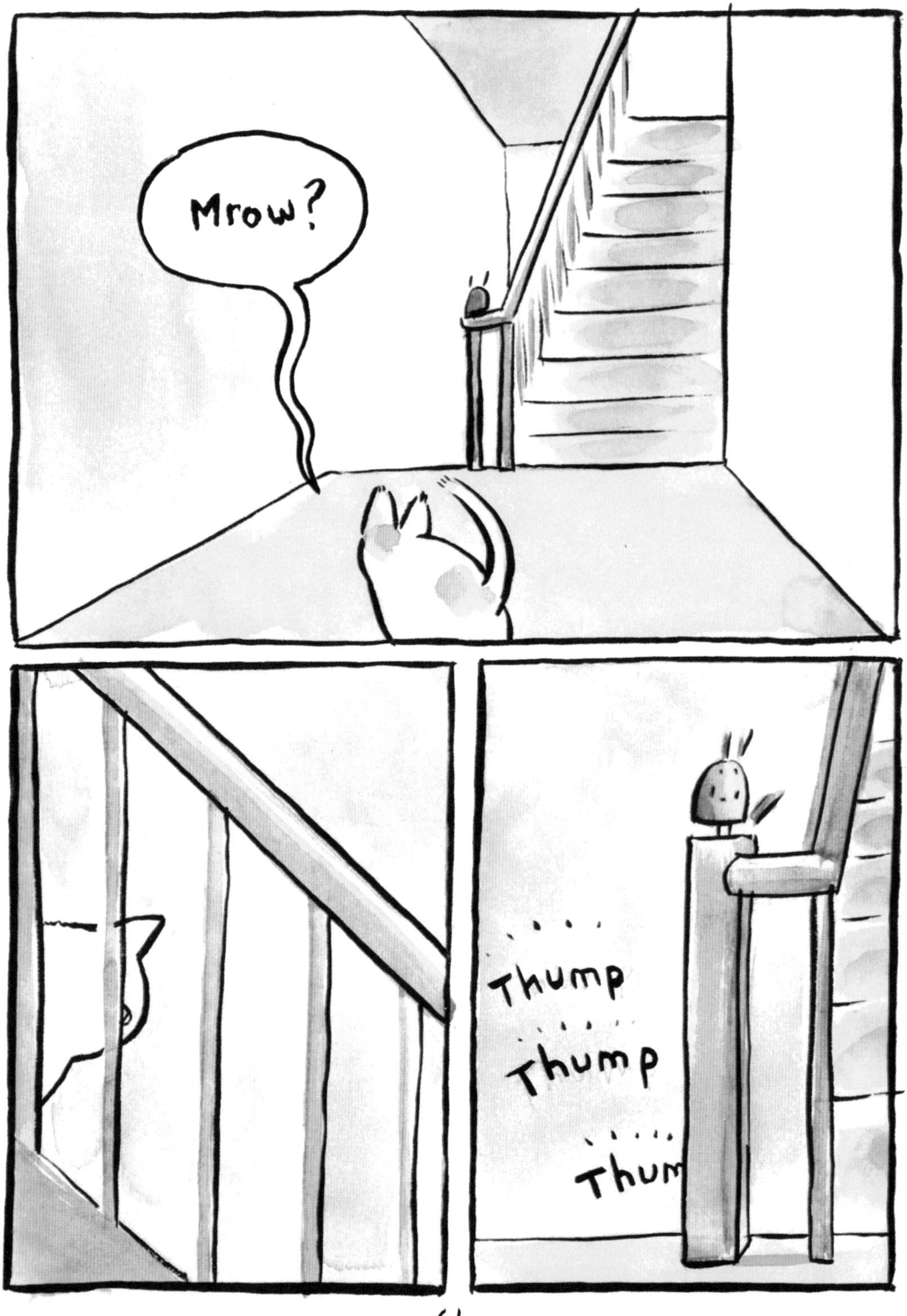
Mrow?
Thump
Thump
Thum

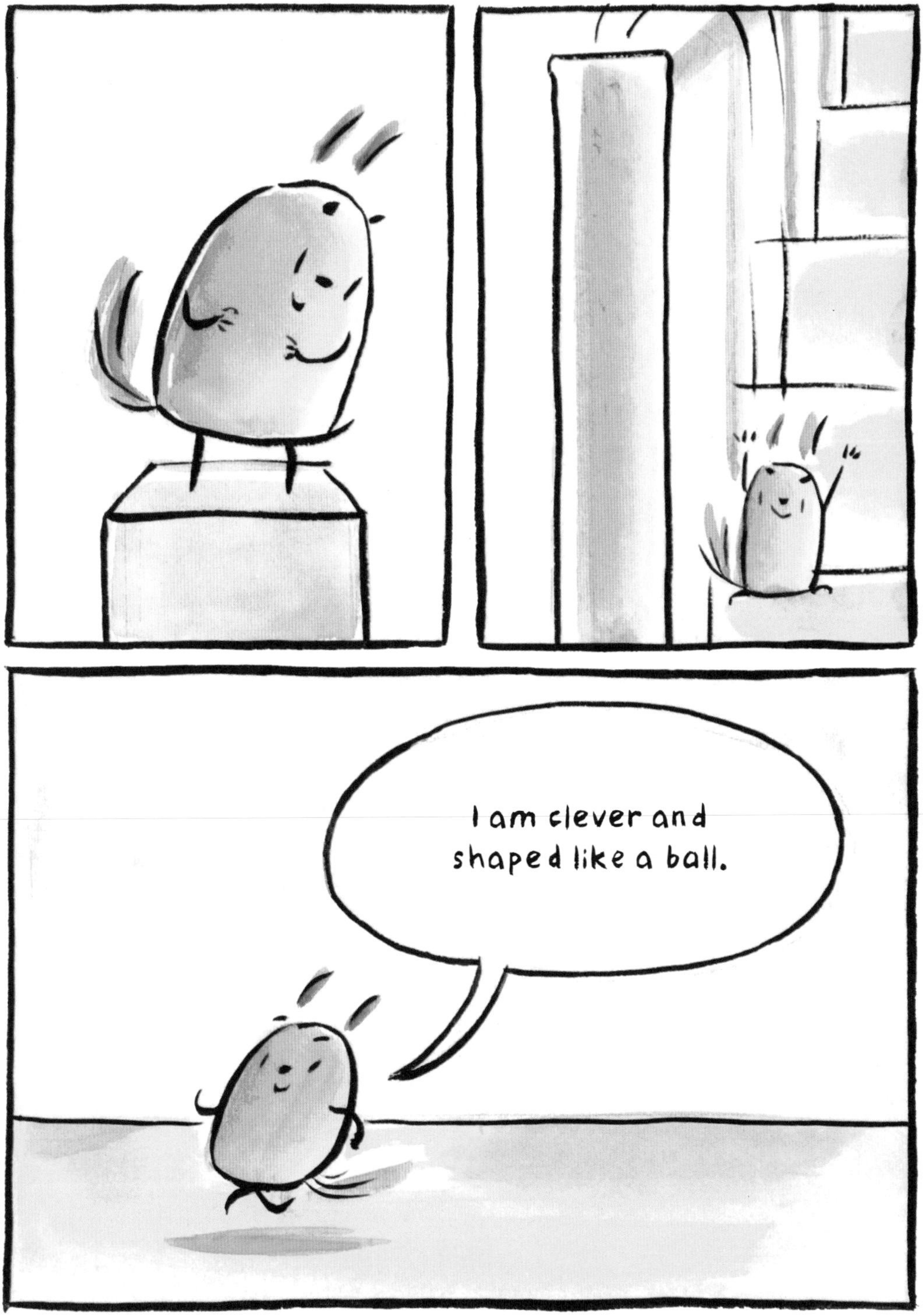
I am clever and shaped like a ball.

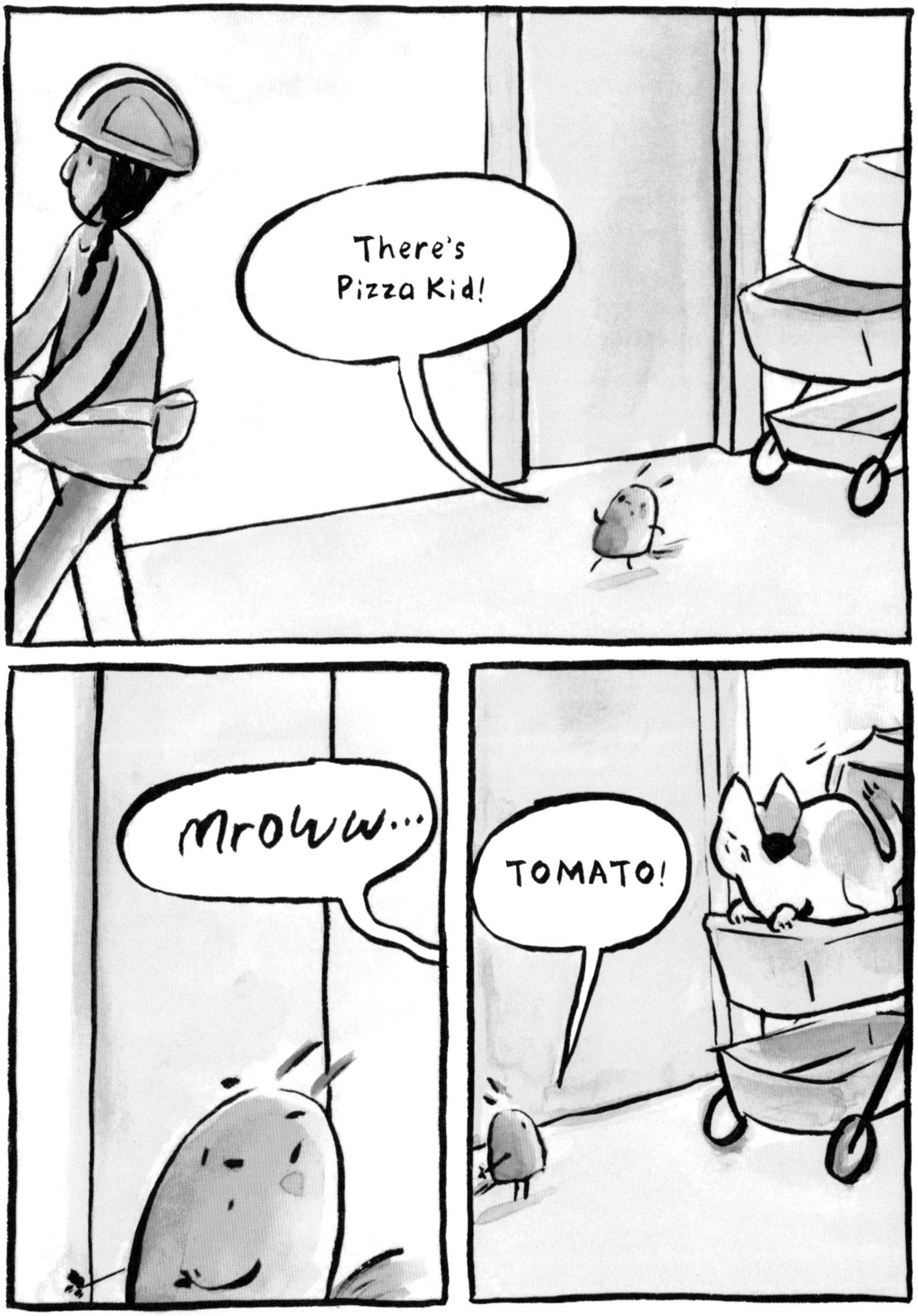
There's Pizza Kid!
Mroww...
TOMATO!

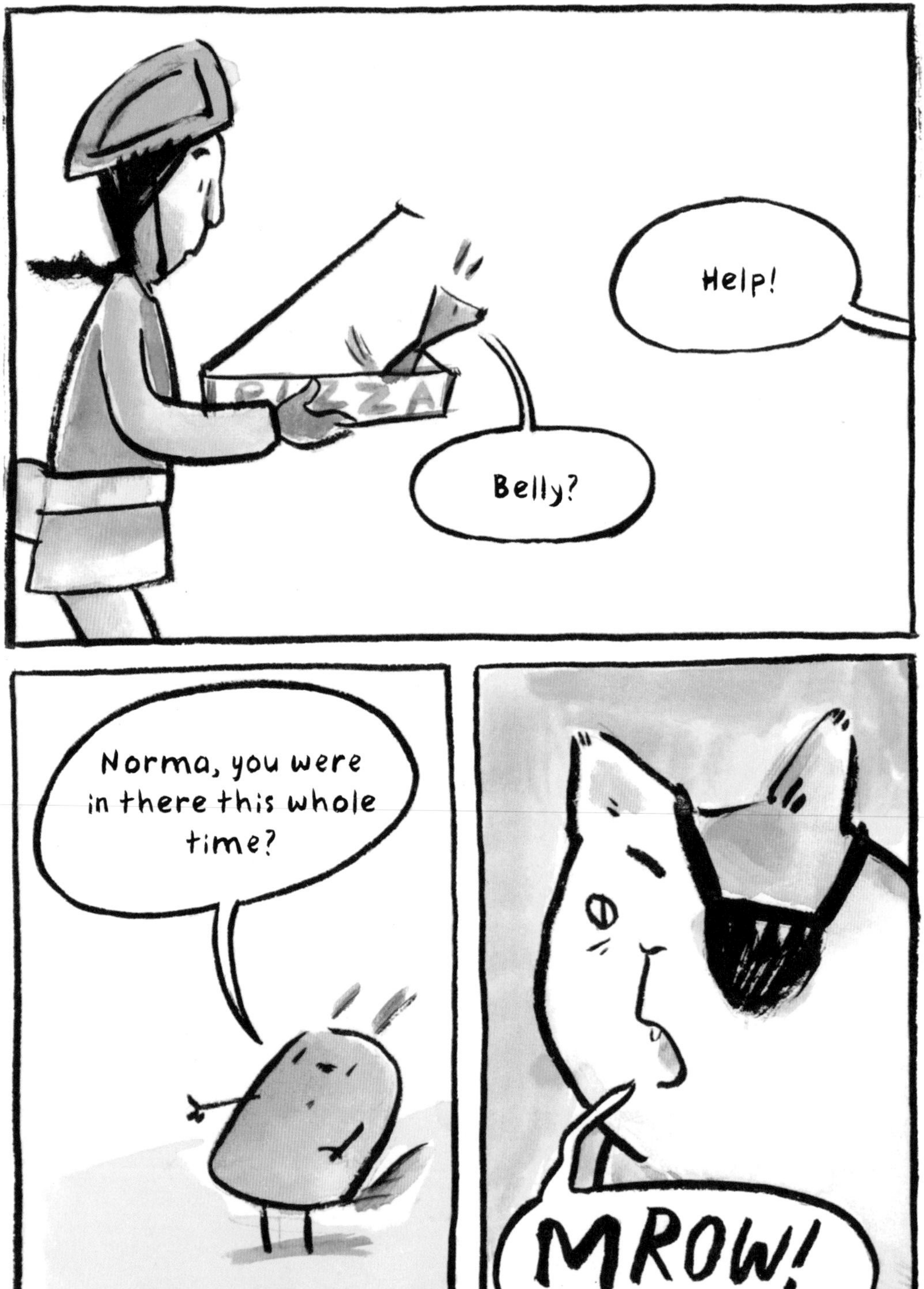
PIZZA
Help!
Belly?
Norma, you were in there this whole time?
MROW!

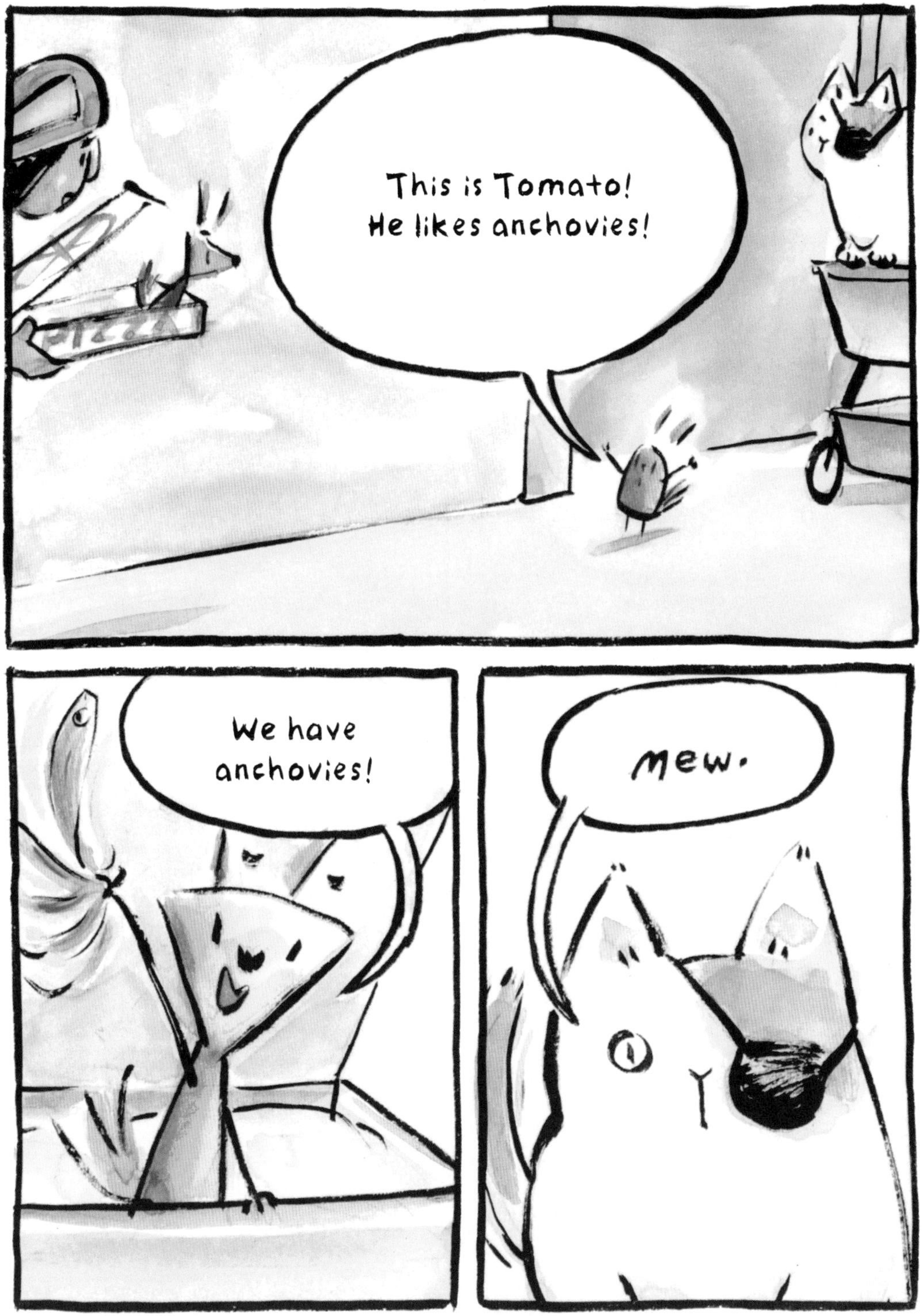
This is Tomato!
He likes anchovies!
We have anchovies!
mew.

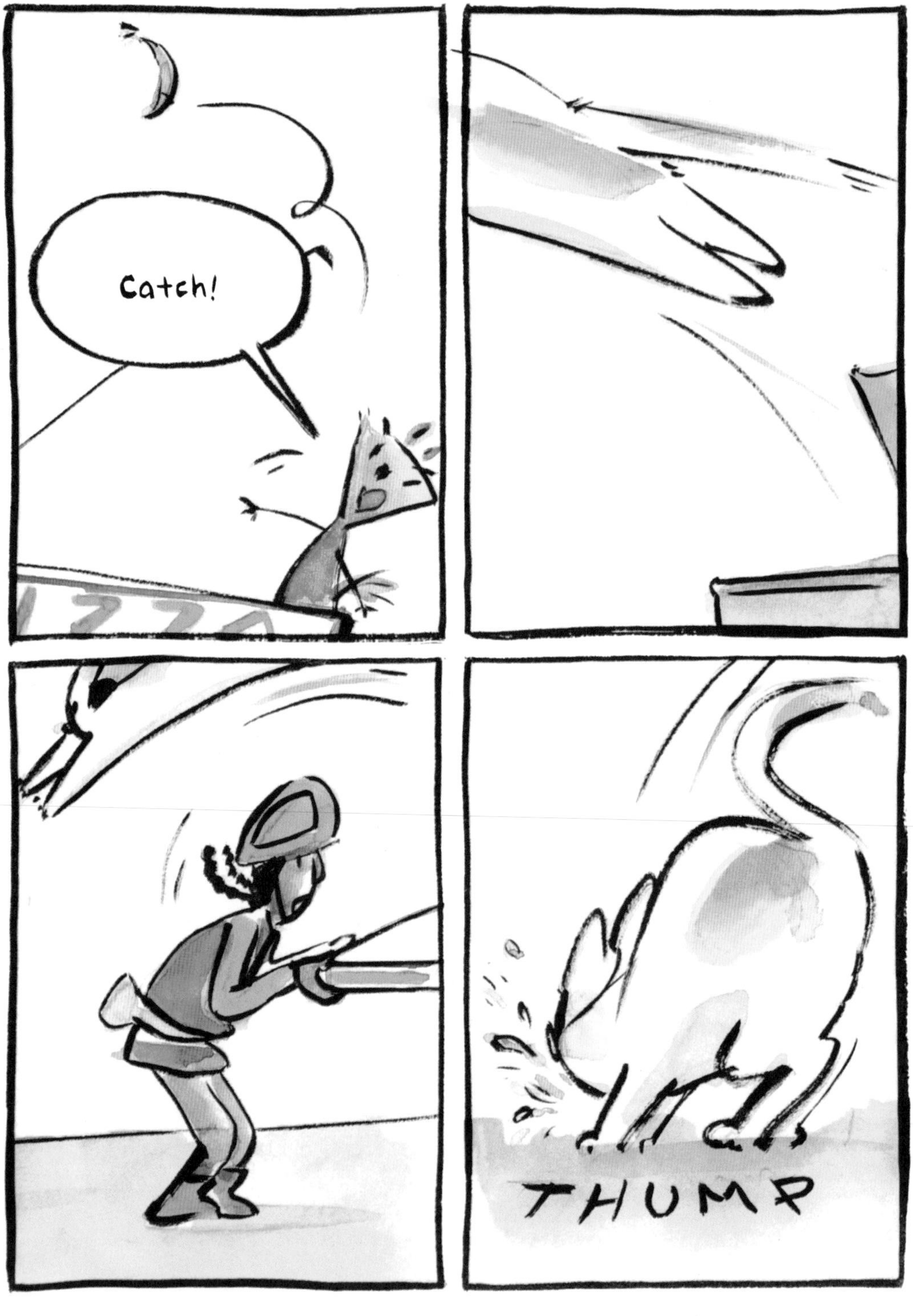
Catch!
THUMP

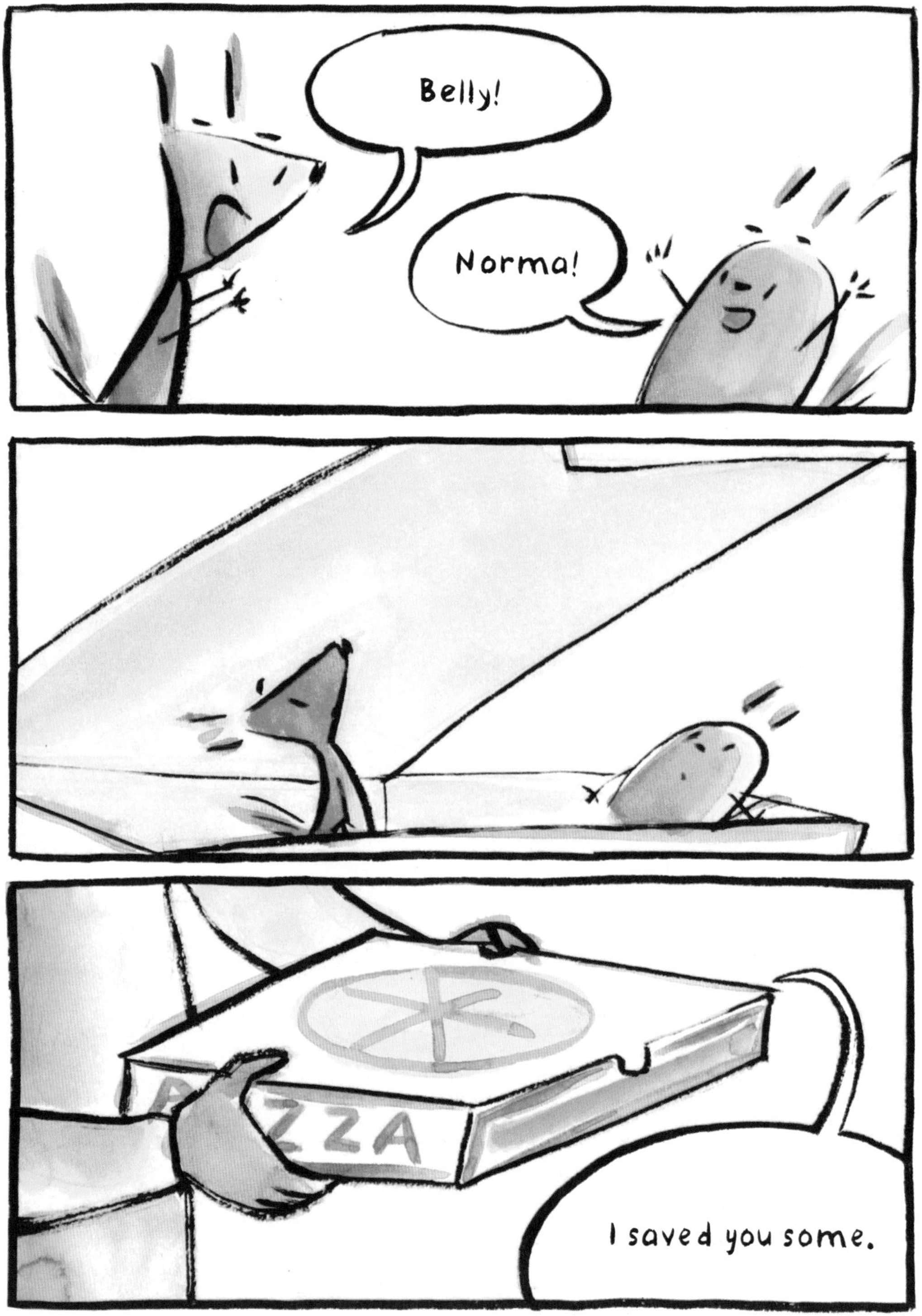
Belly!
Norma!
PIZZA
I saved you some.

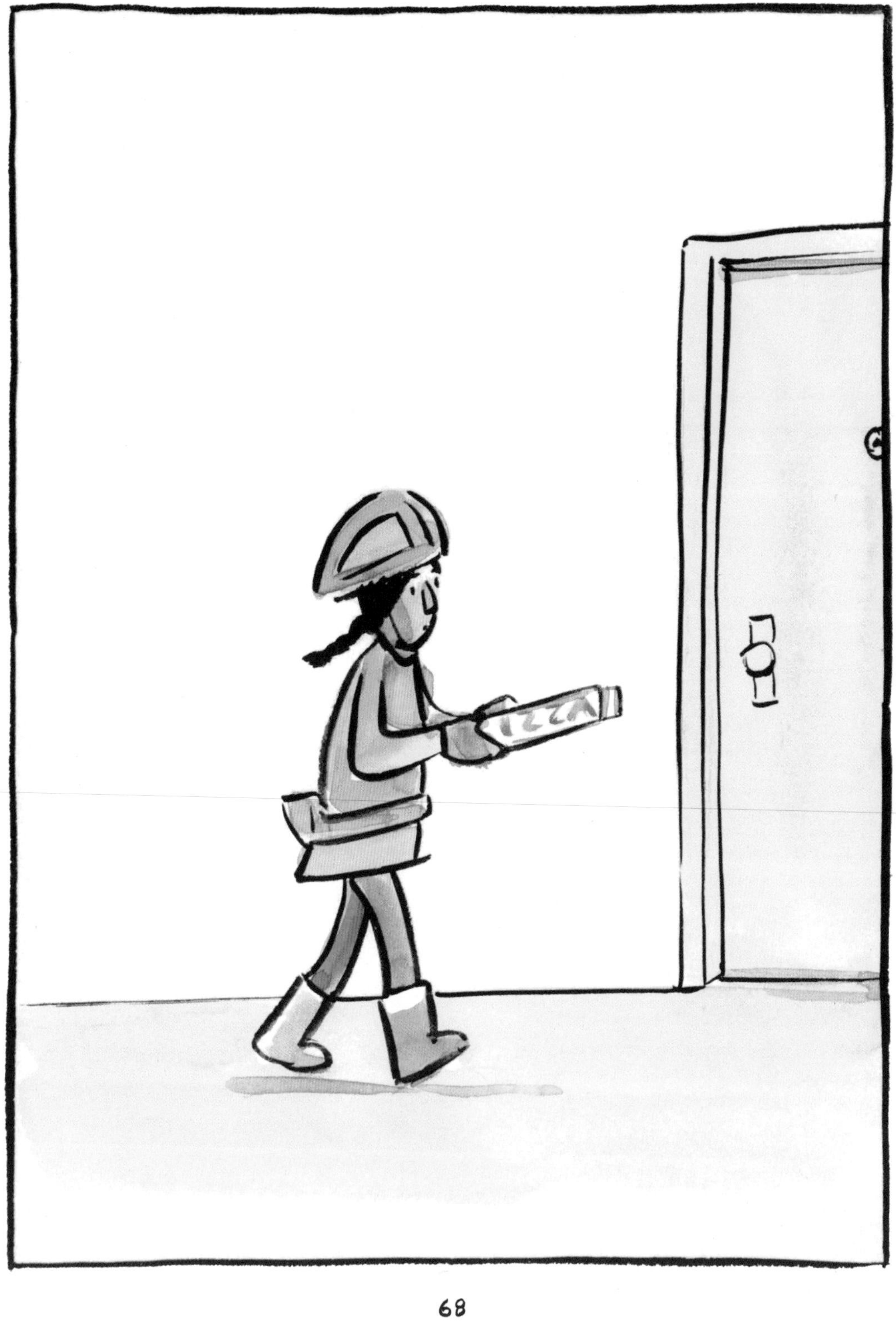
IZZA

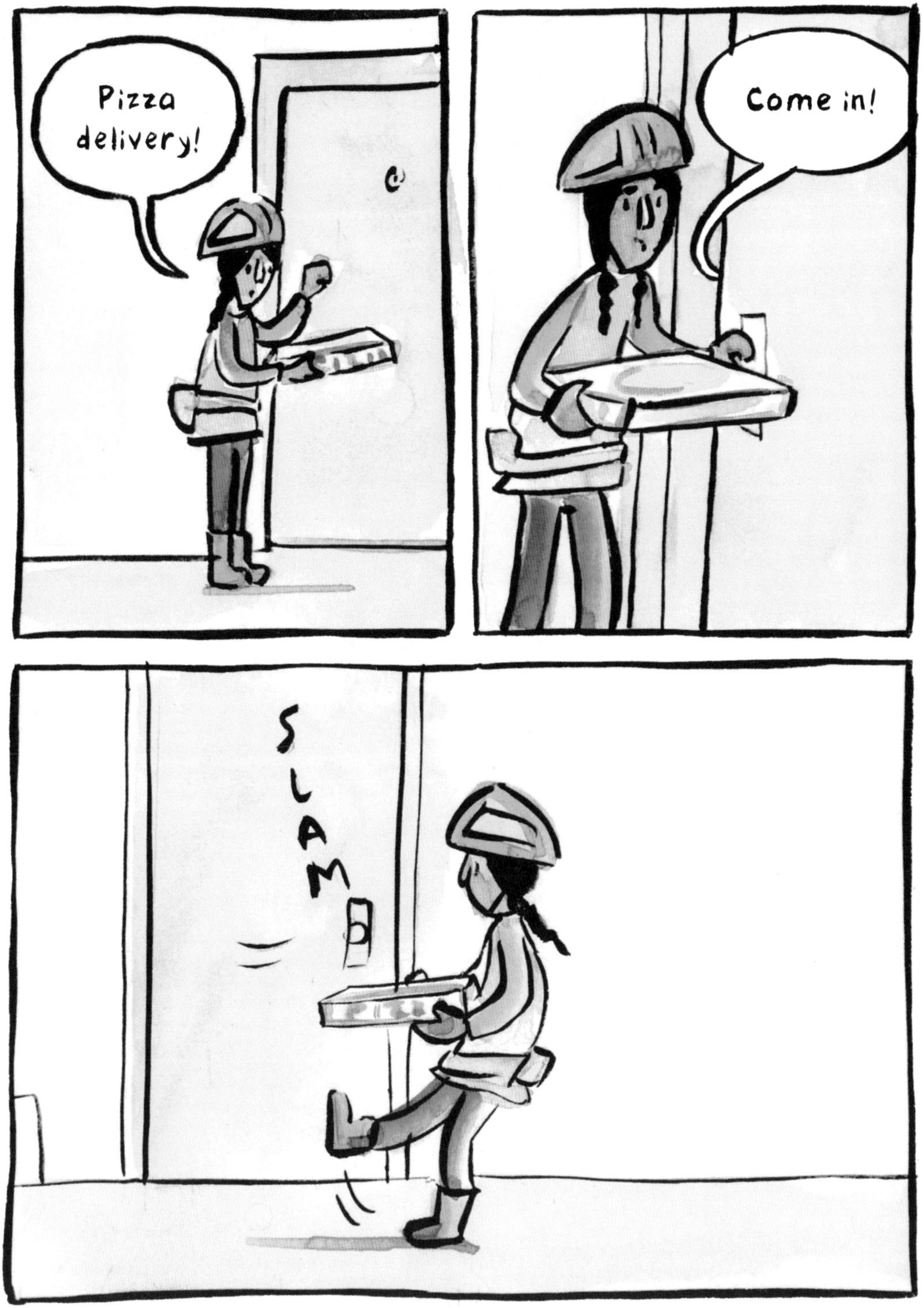
Pizza delivery!
Come in!
SLAM

chapter 7

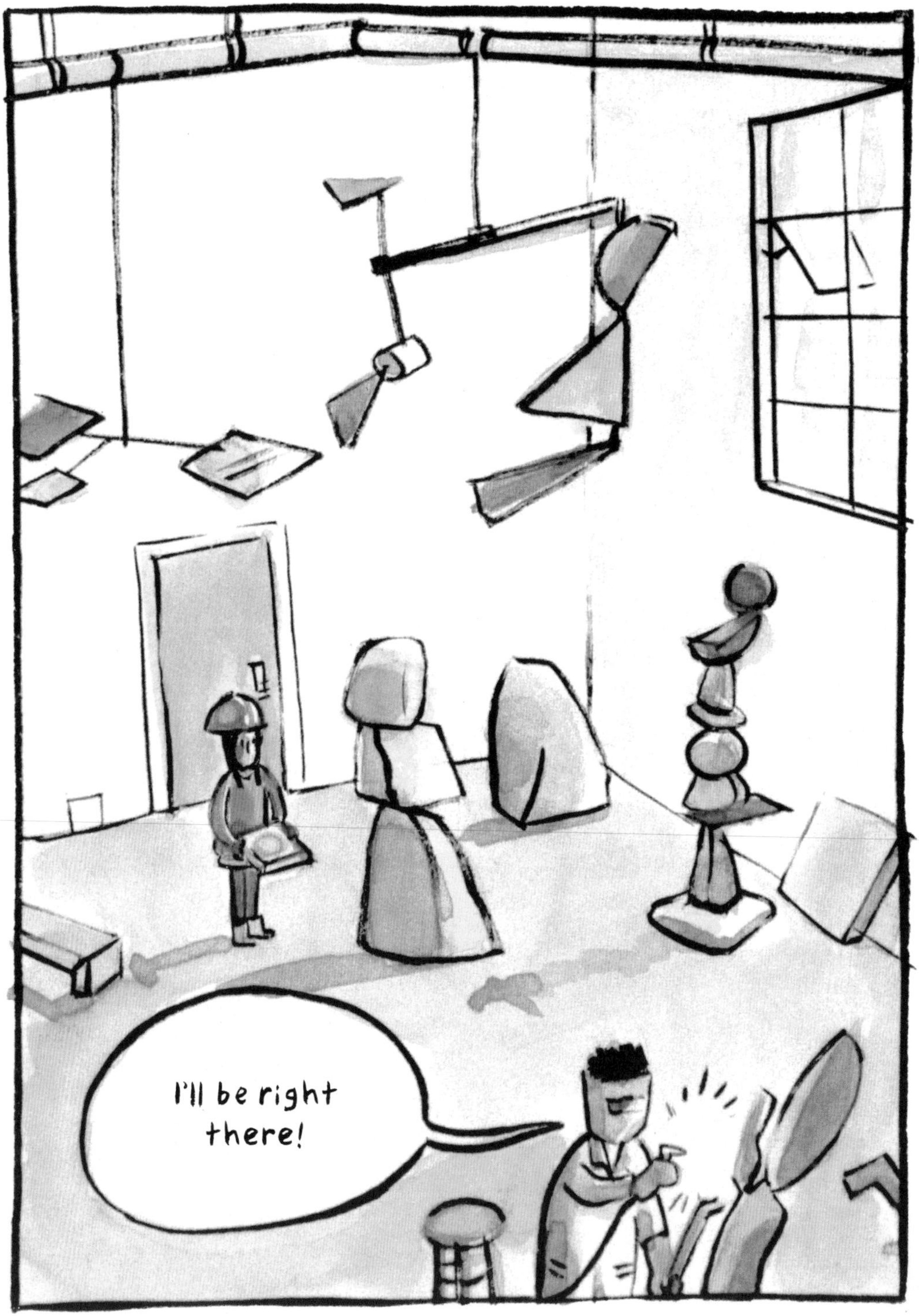
I'll be right there!

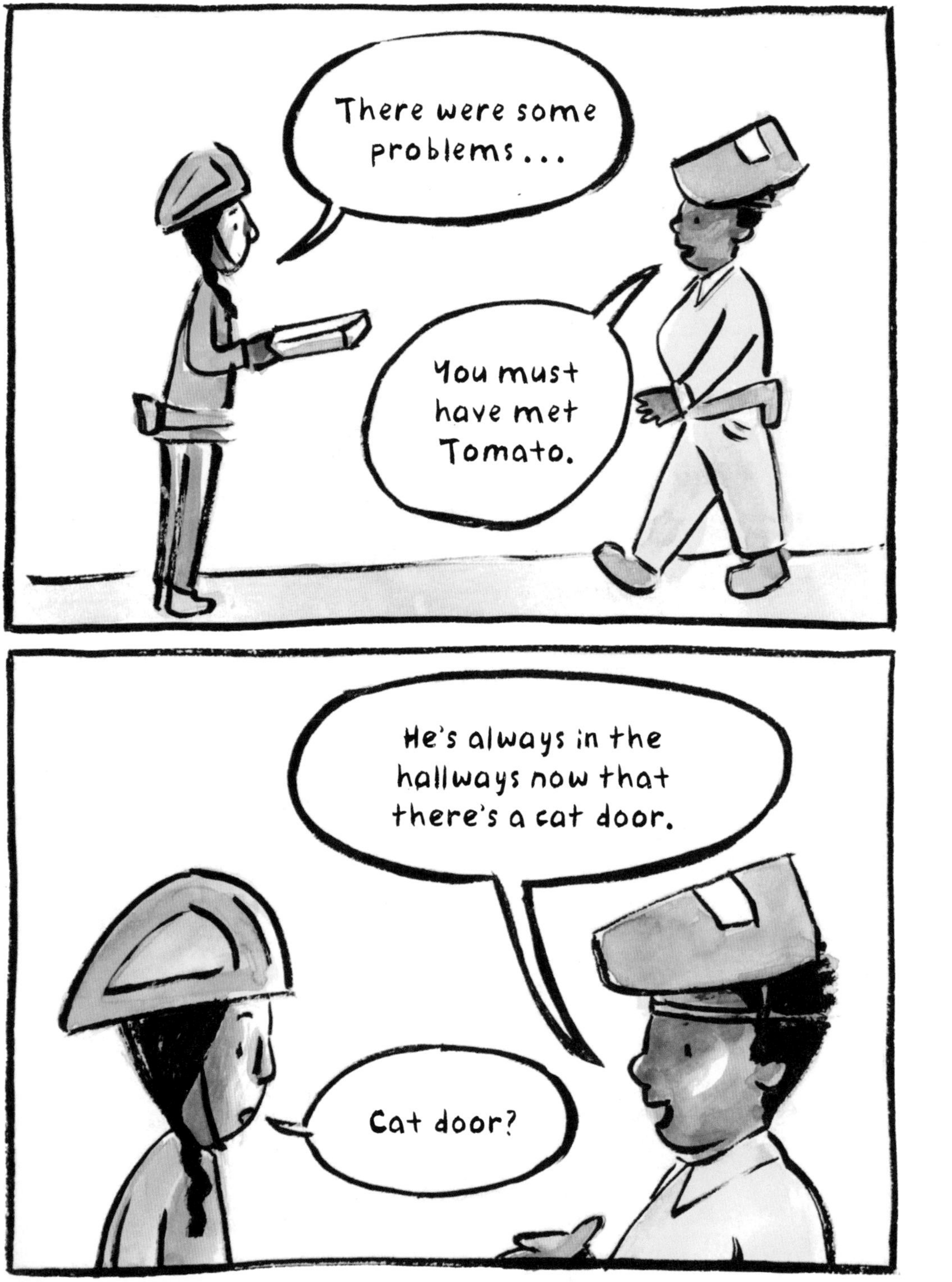
There were some problems...
You must have met Tomato.
He's always in the hallways now that there's a cat door.
Cat door?

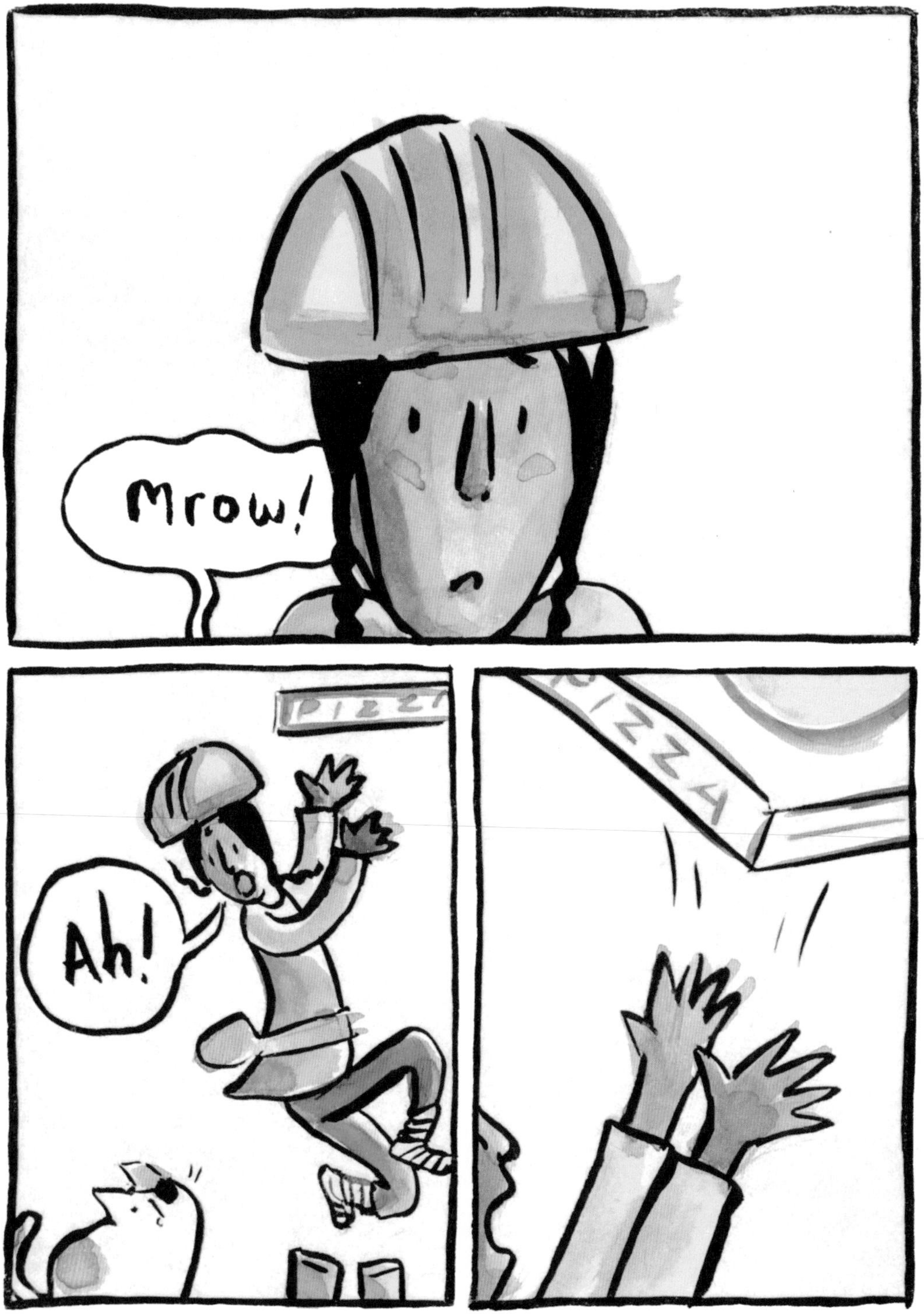
Mrow!
Ah!
PIZZ
PIZZA

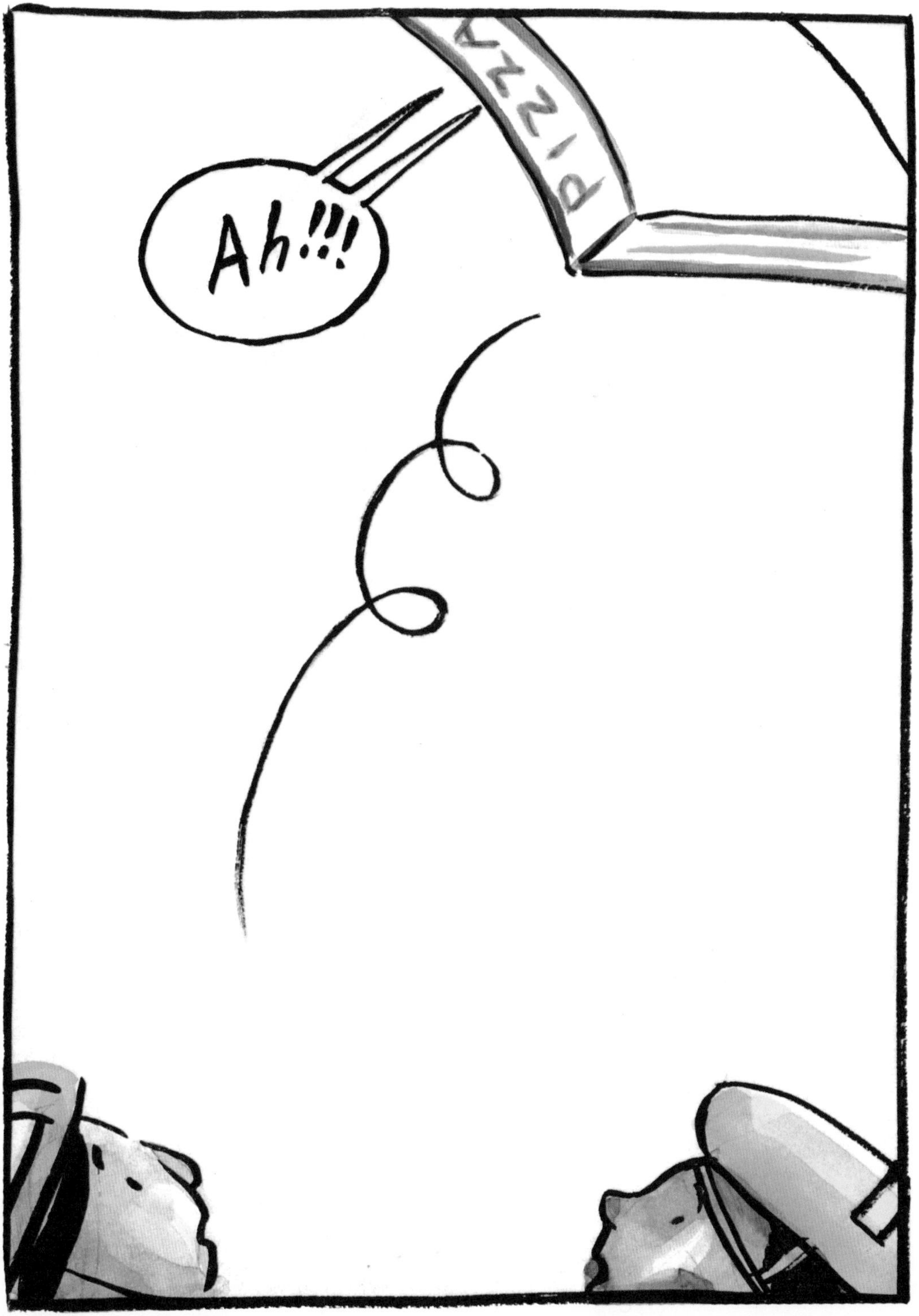

Ah!!!
PIZZA

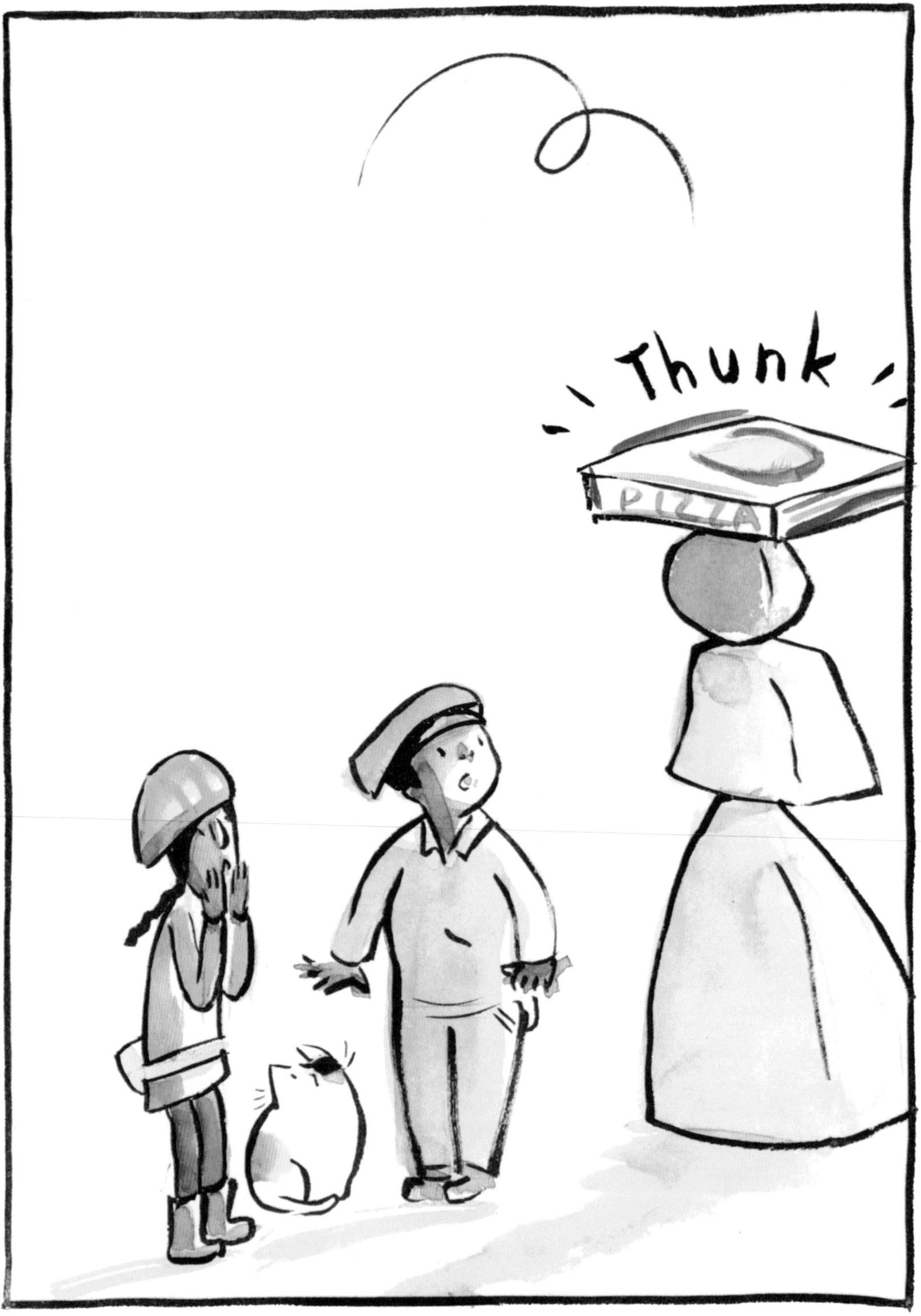
Thunk
PIZZA

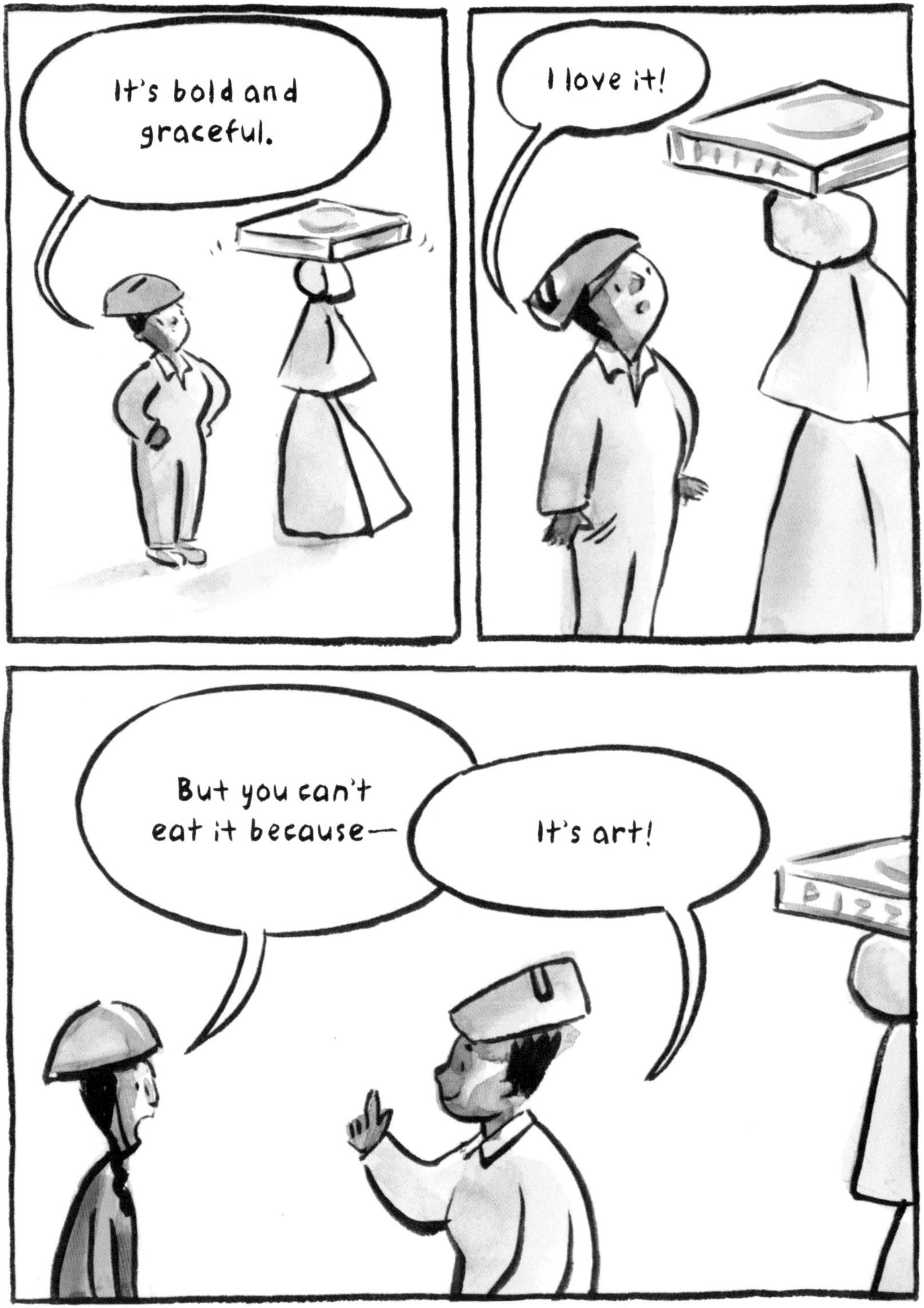
It's bold and graceful.
I love it!
But you can't eat it because—
It's art!

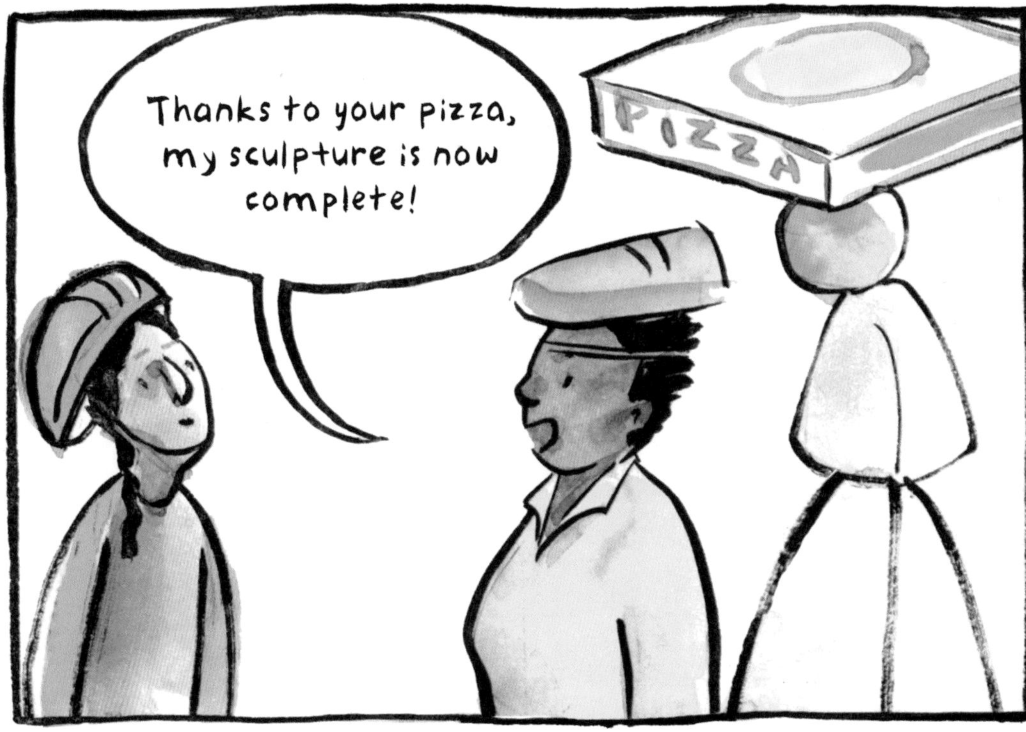
Thanks to your pizza, my sculpture is now complete!
PIZZA

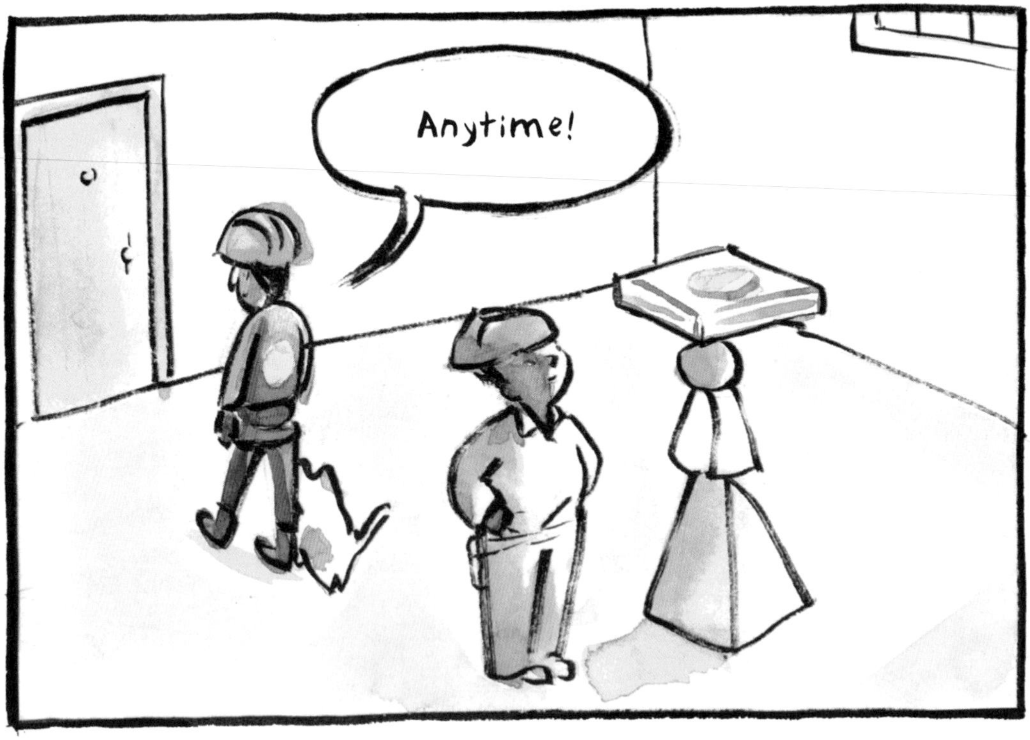
Anytime!

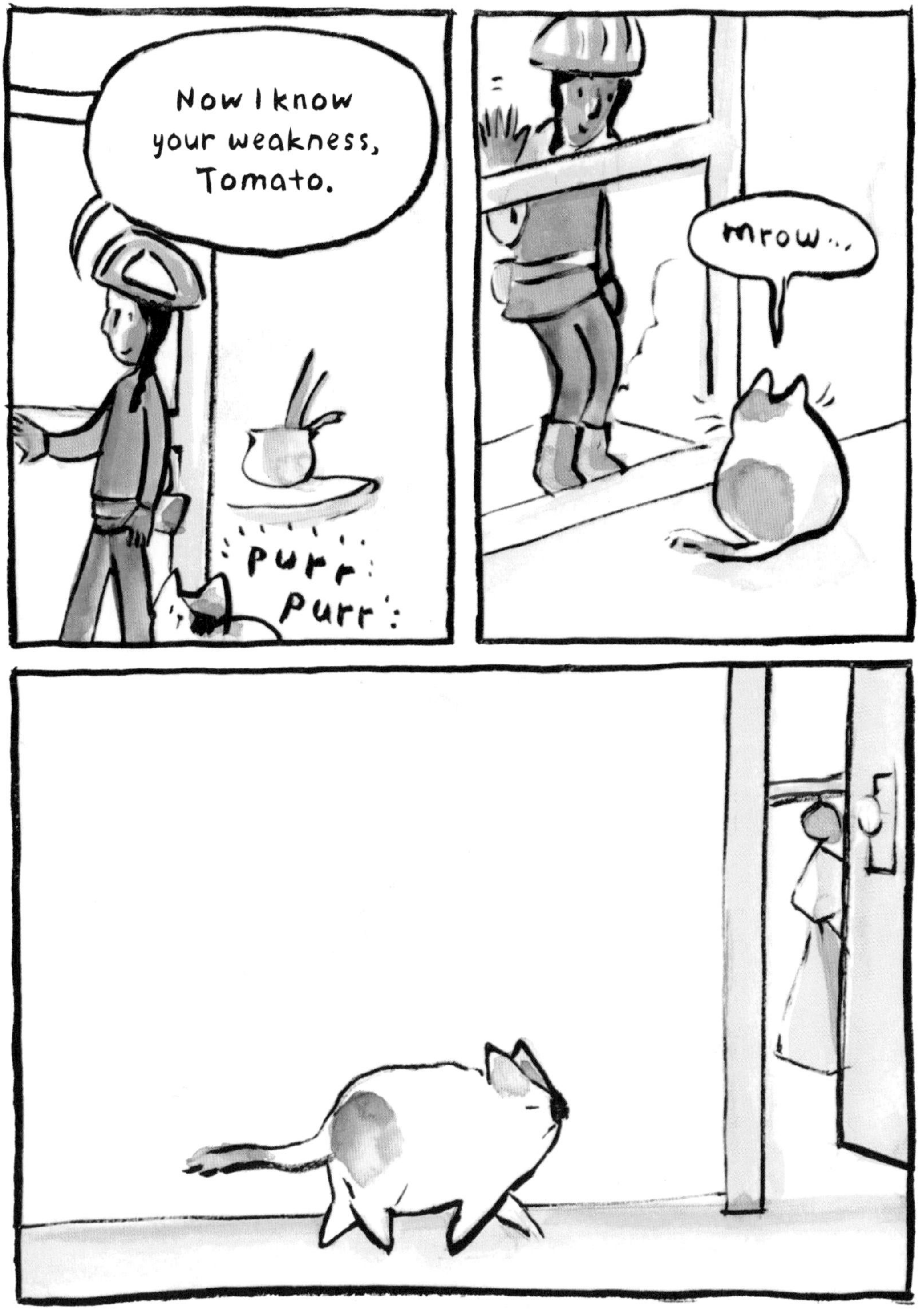
Now I know your weakness, Tomato.
purr purr
mrow...

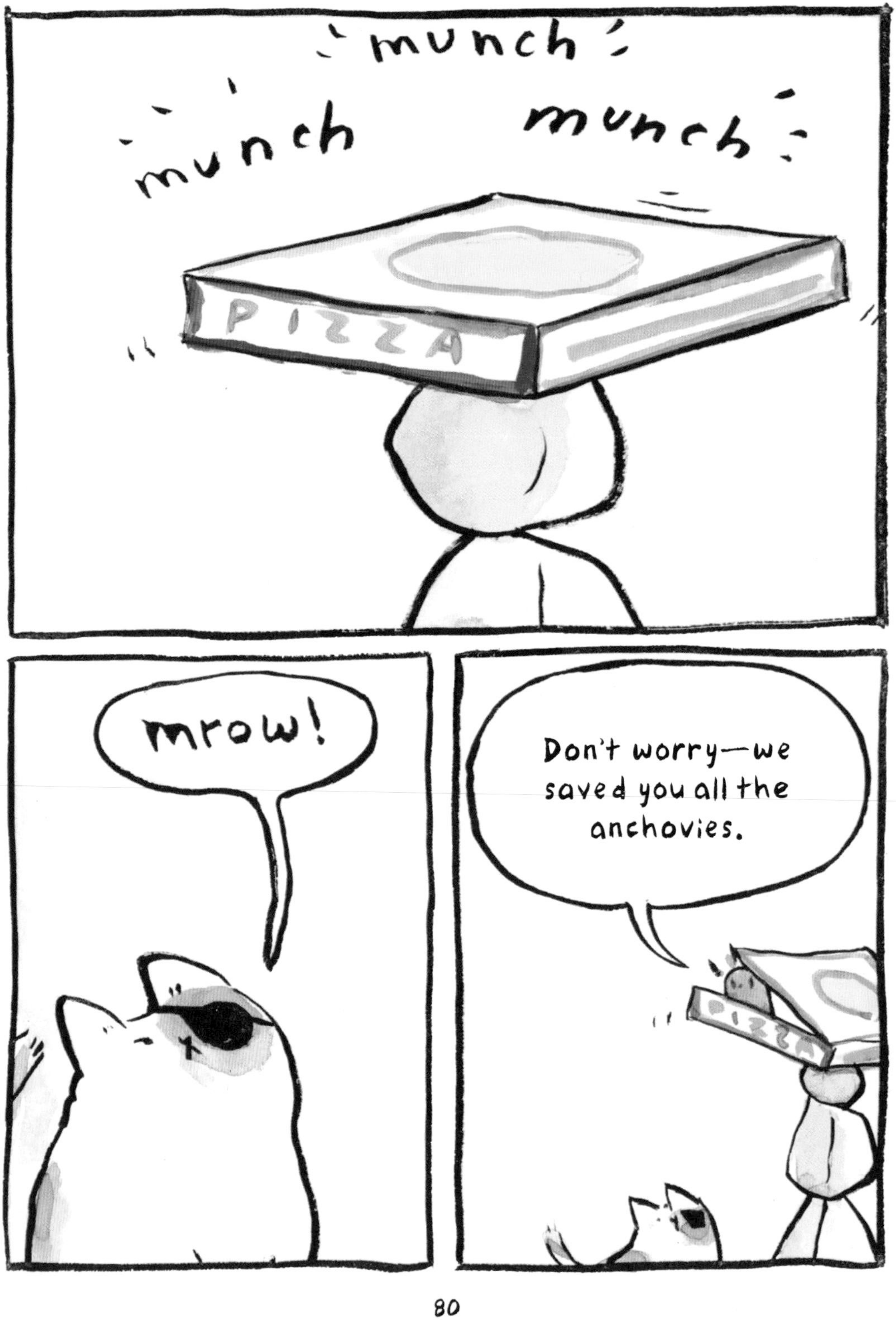
munch
munch
munch
PIZZA
mrow!
Don't worry—we saved you all the anchovies.
PIZZA

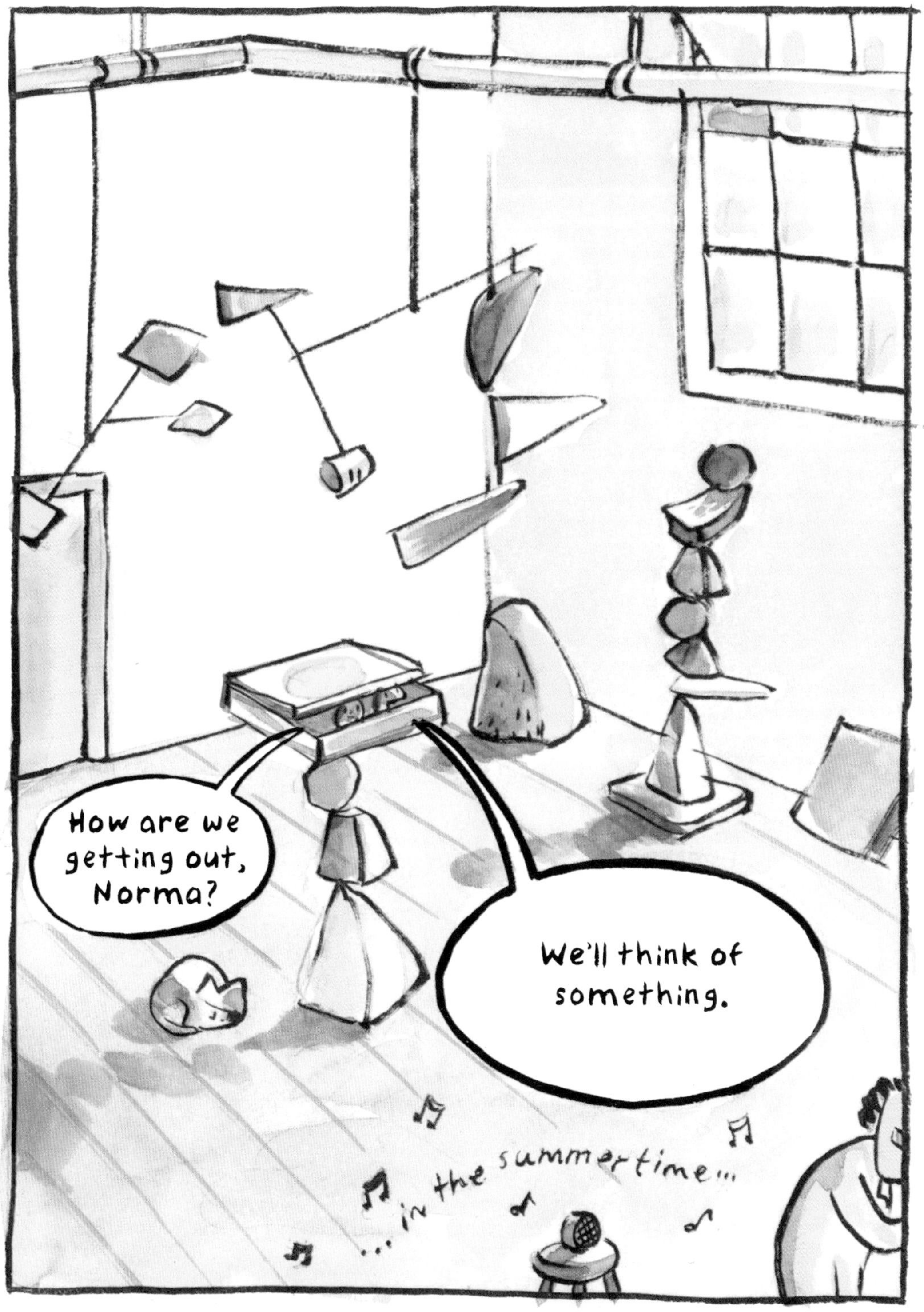
How are we getting out, Norma?
We'll think of something.
... in the summertime...

chapter 8

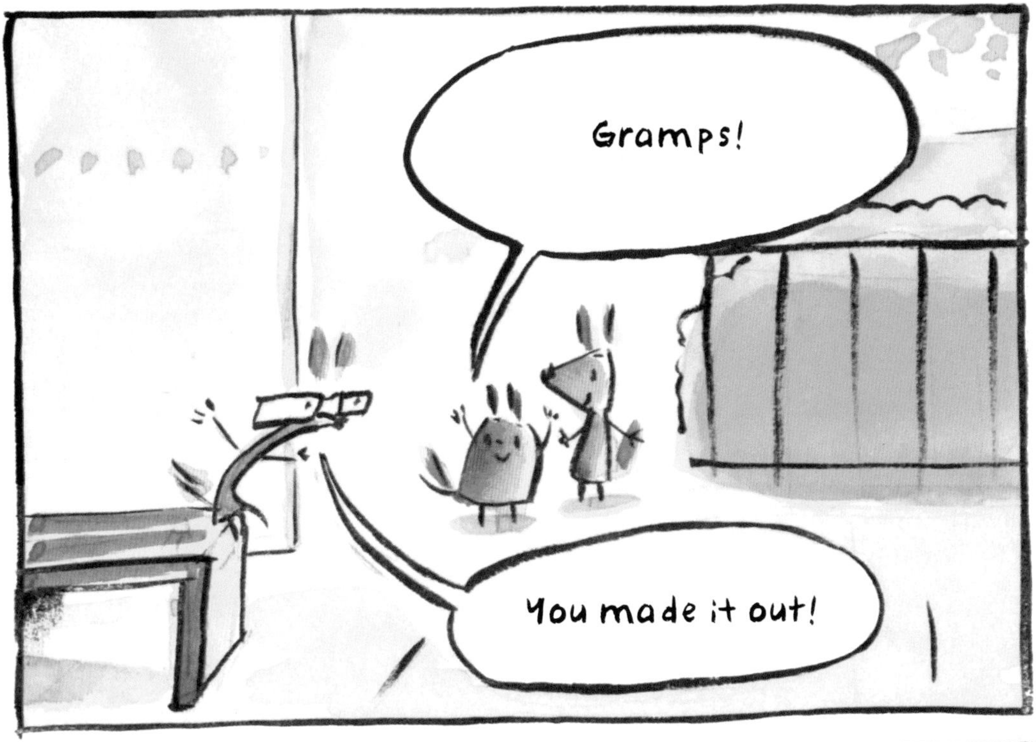
Gramps!
You made it out!

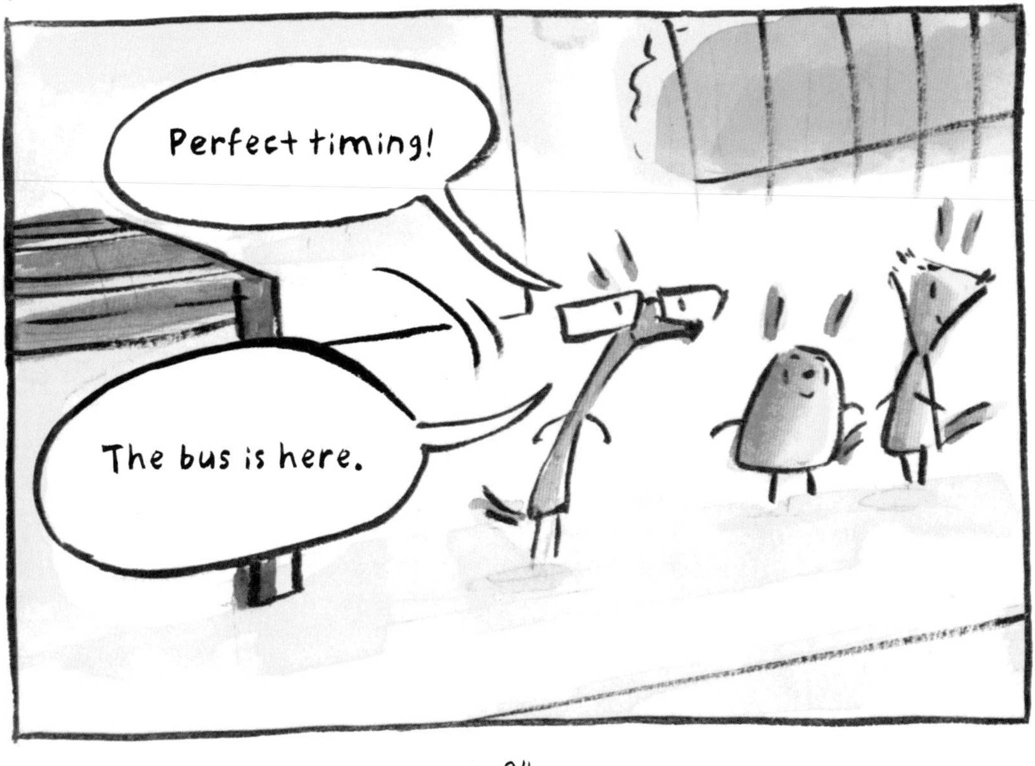
Perfect timing!
The bus is here.

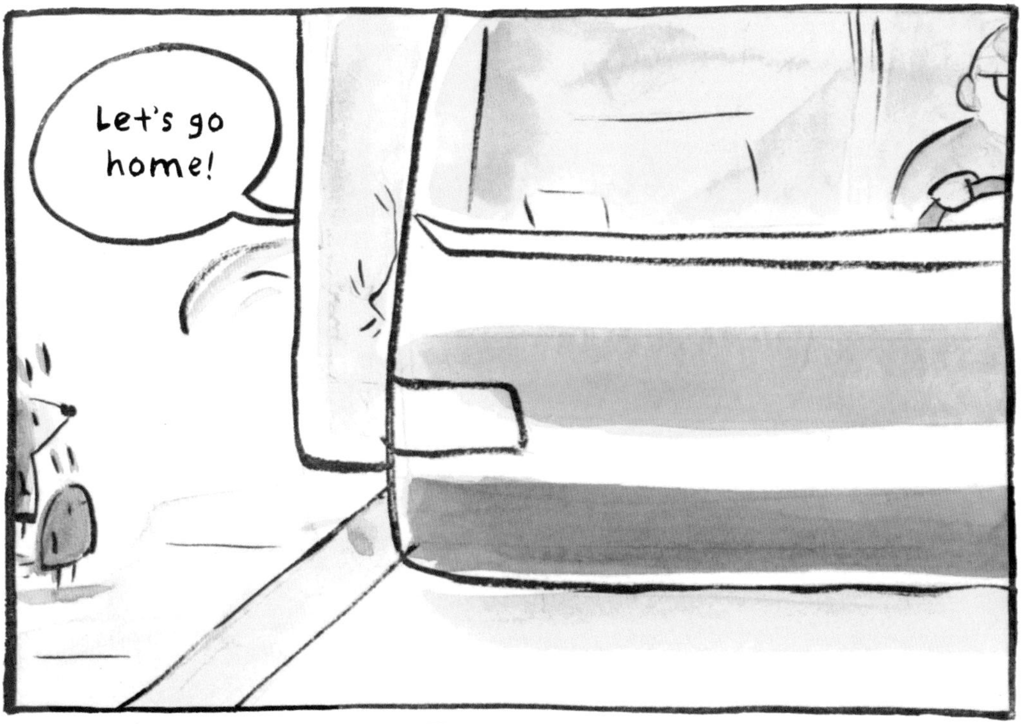
Let's go home!

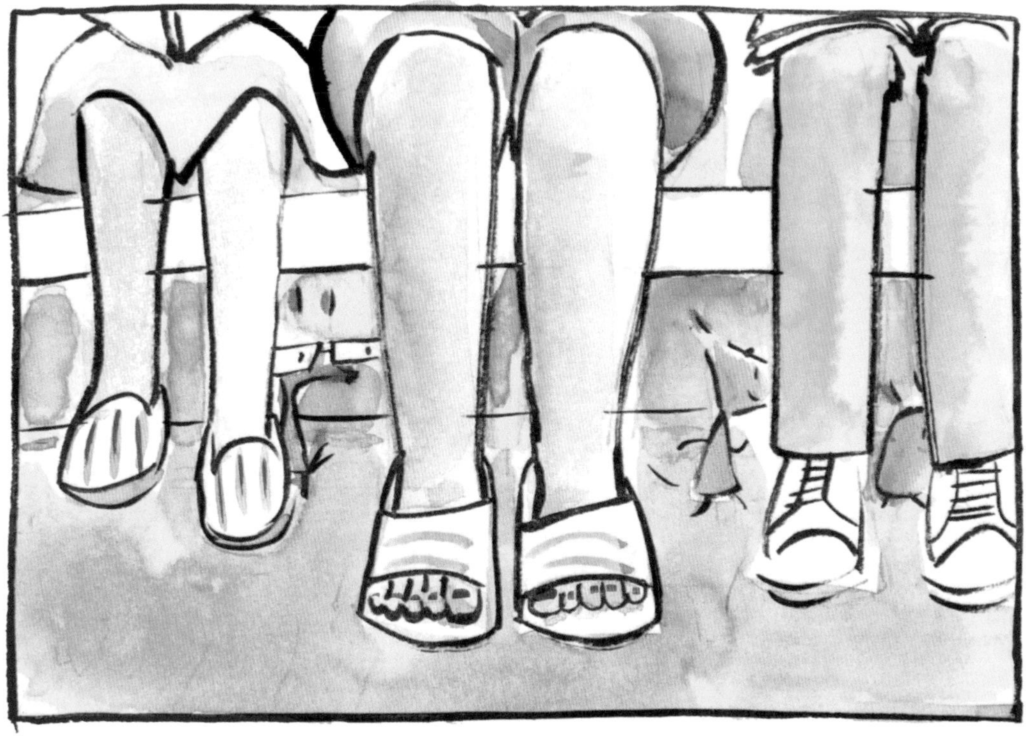

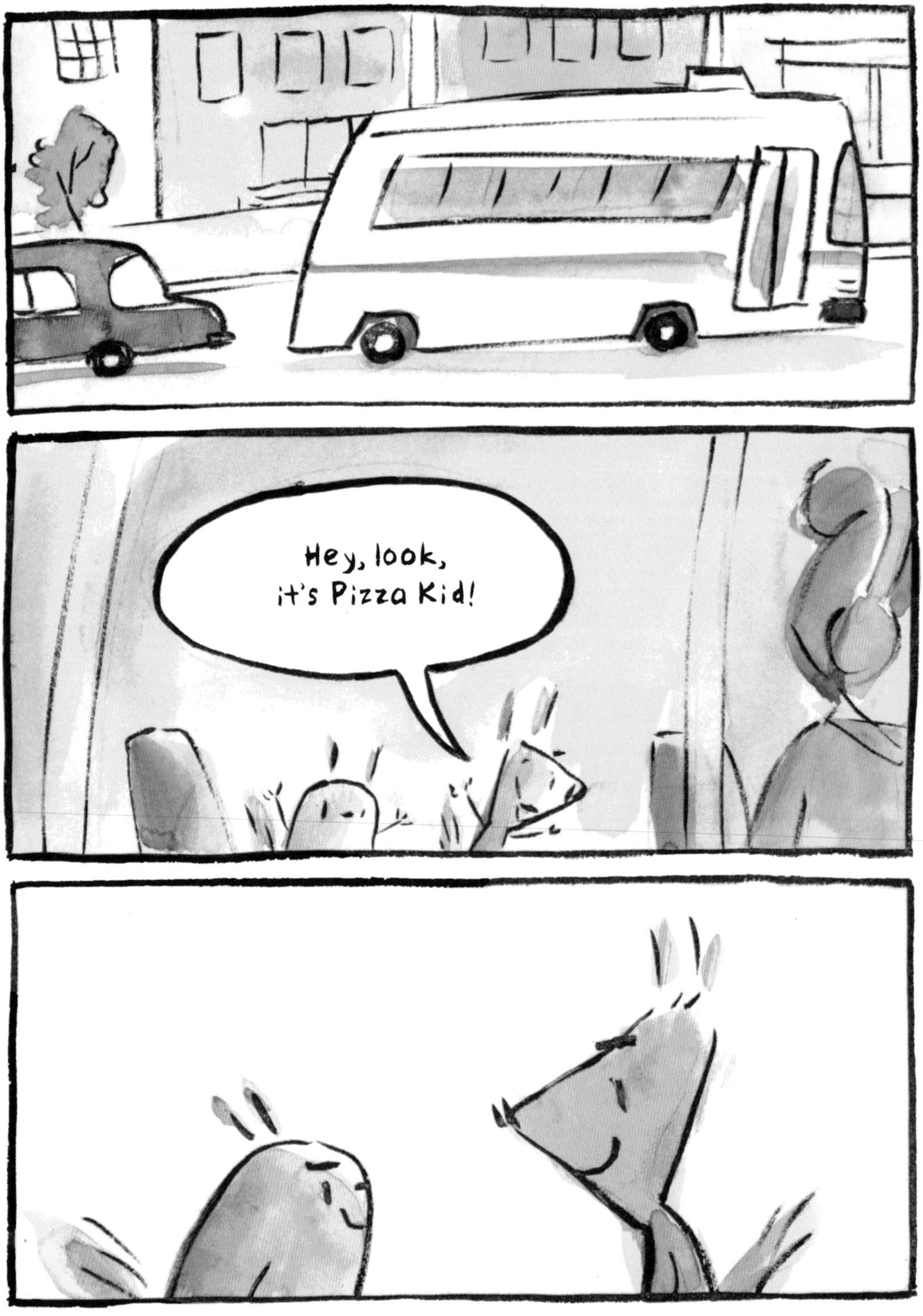
Hey, look,
it's Pizza Kid!

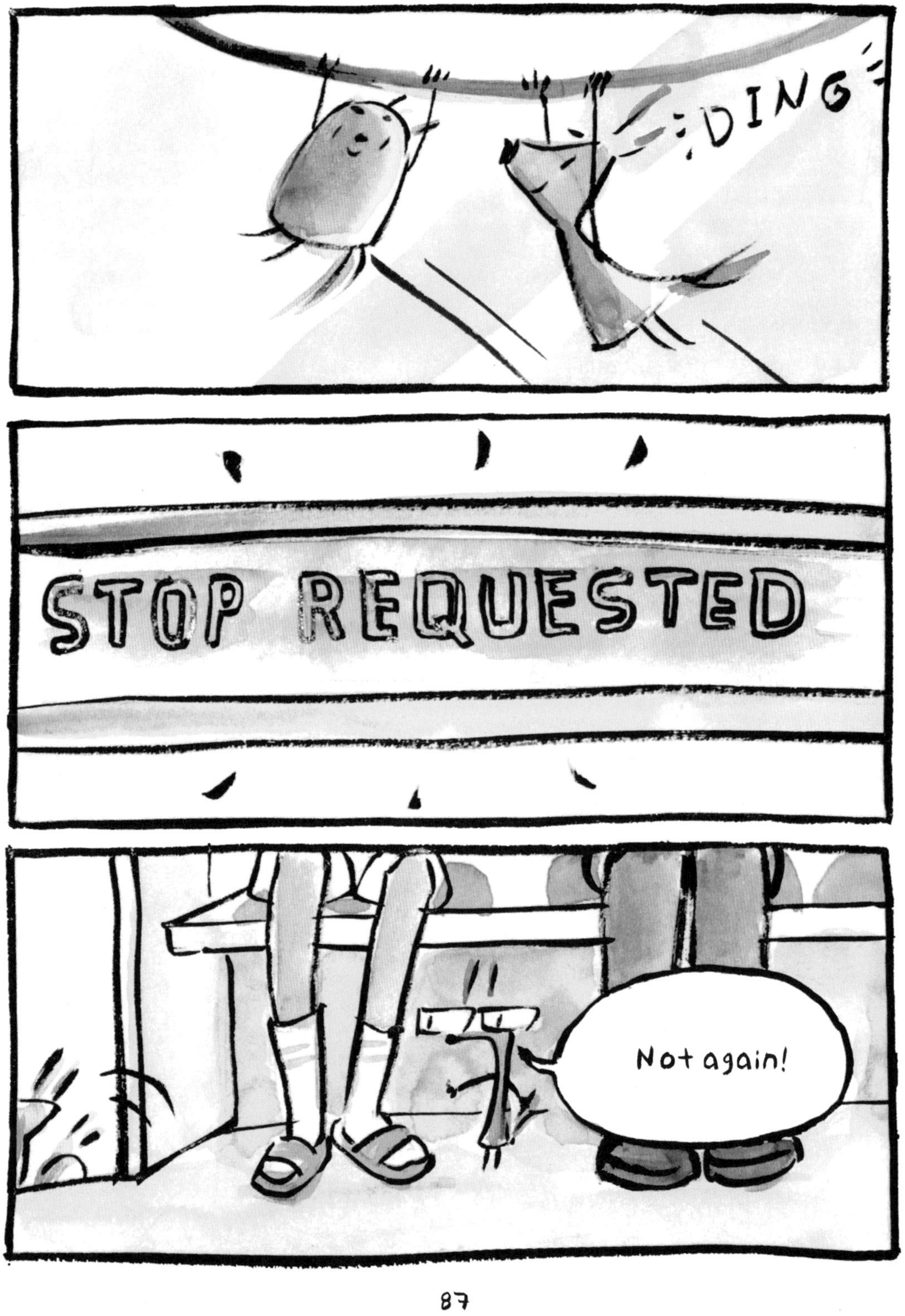
DING
STOP REQUESTED
Not again!

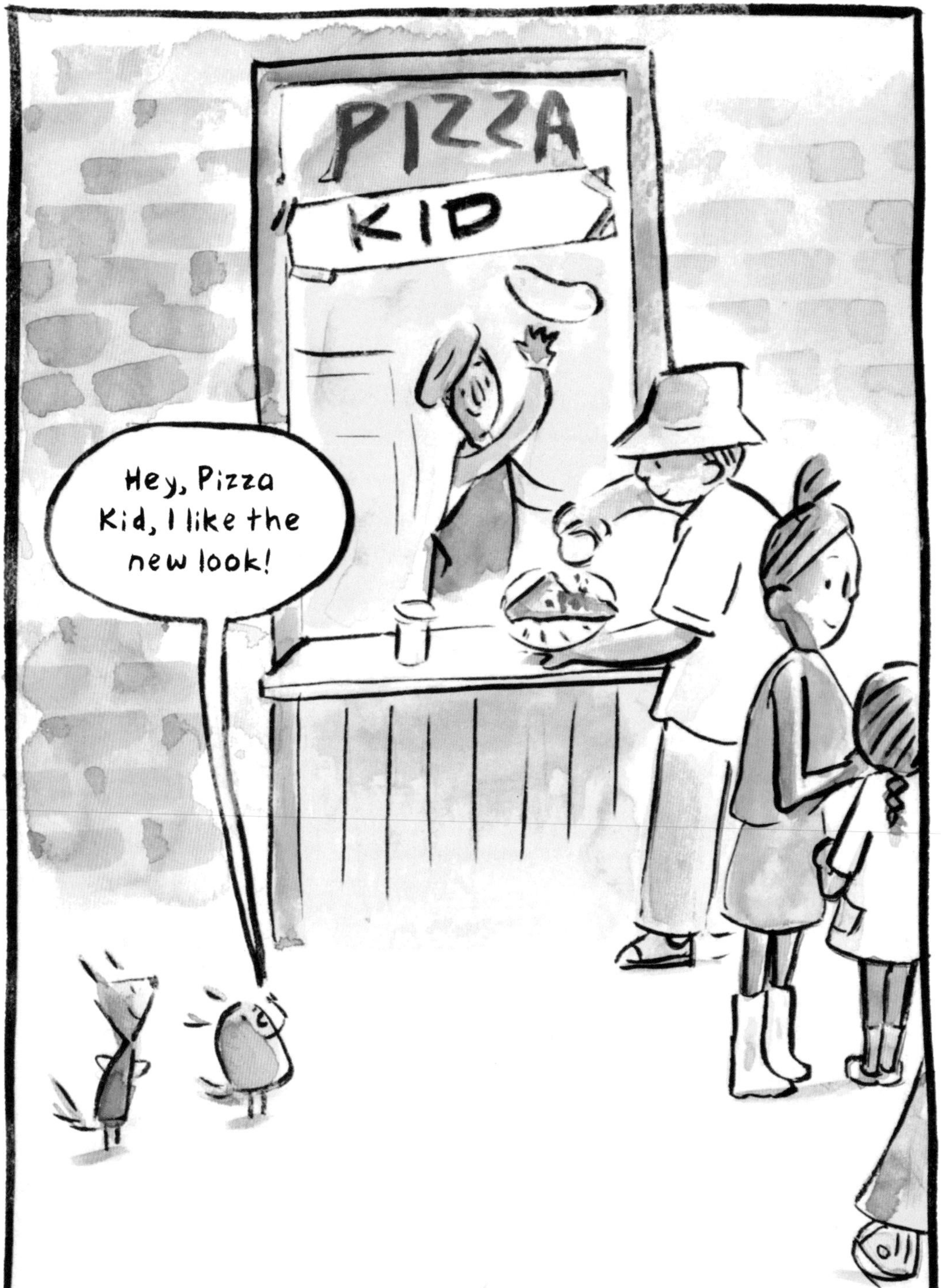
PIZZA
KID
Hey, Pizza Kid, I like the new look!

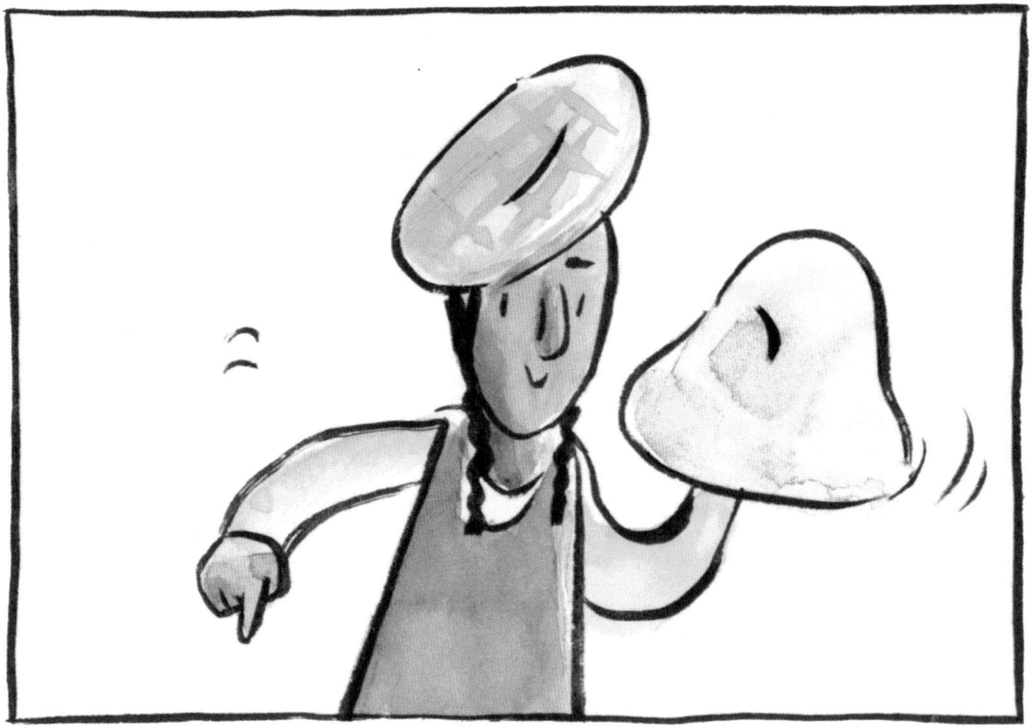

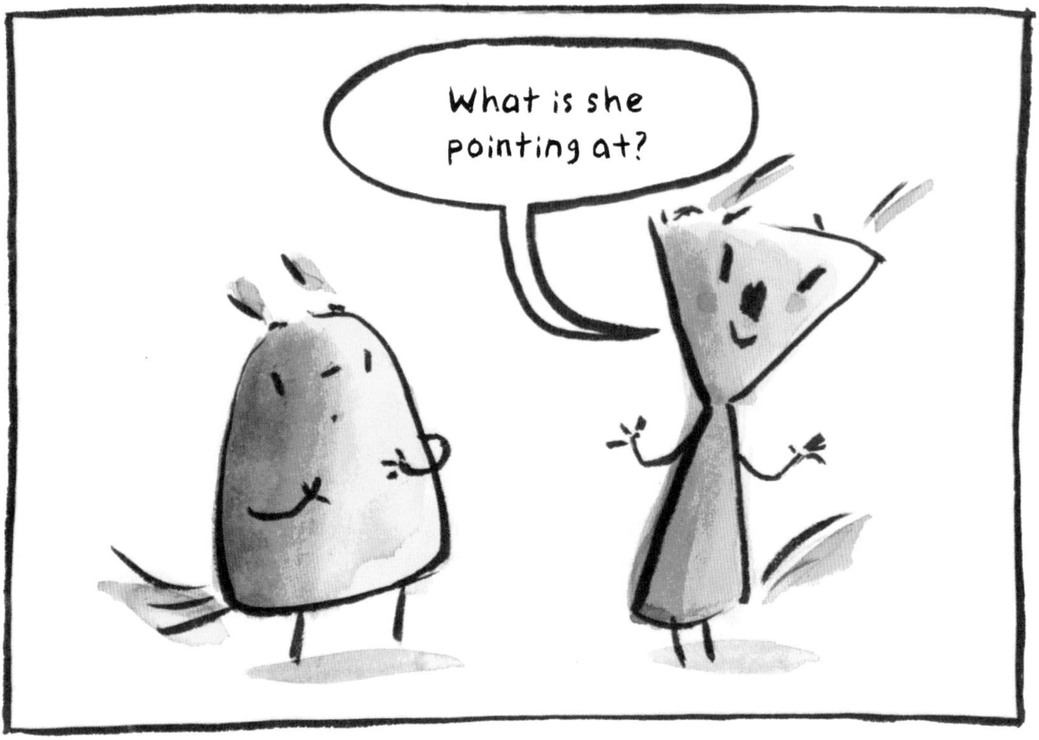
What is she pointing at?

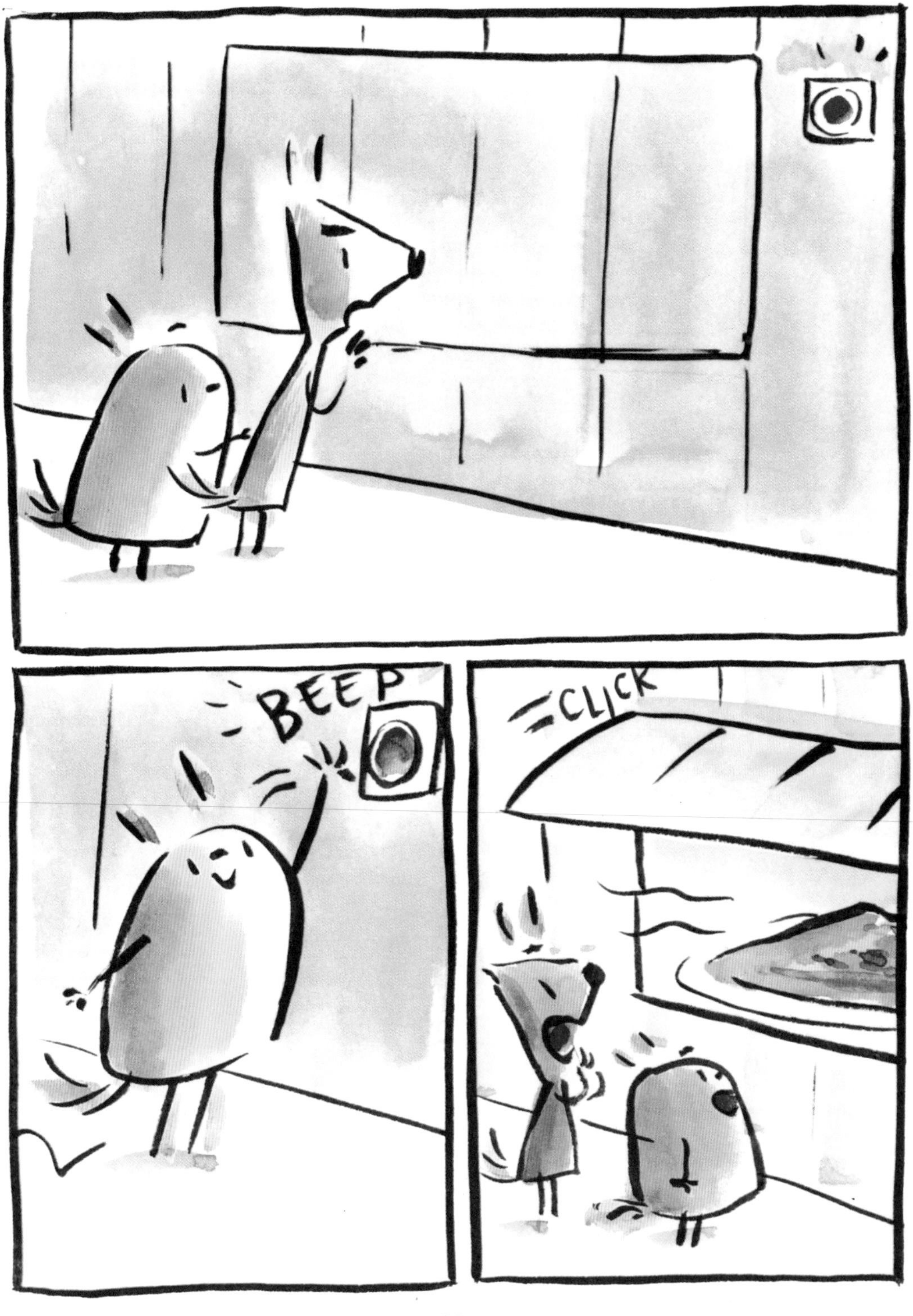
BEEP
CLICK

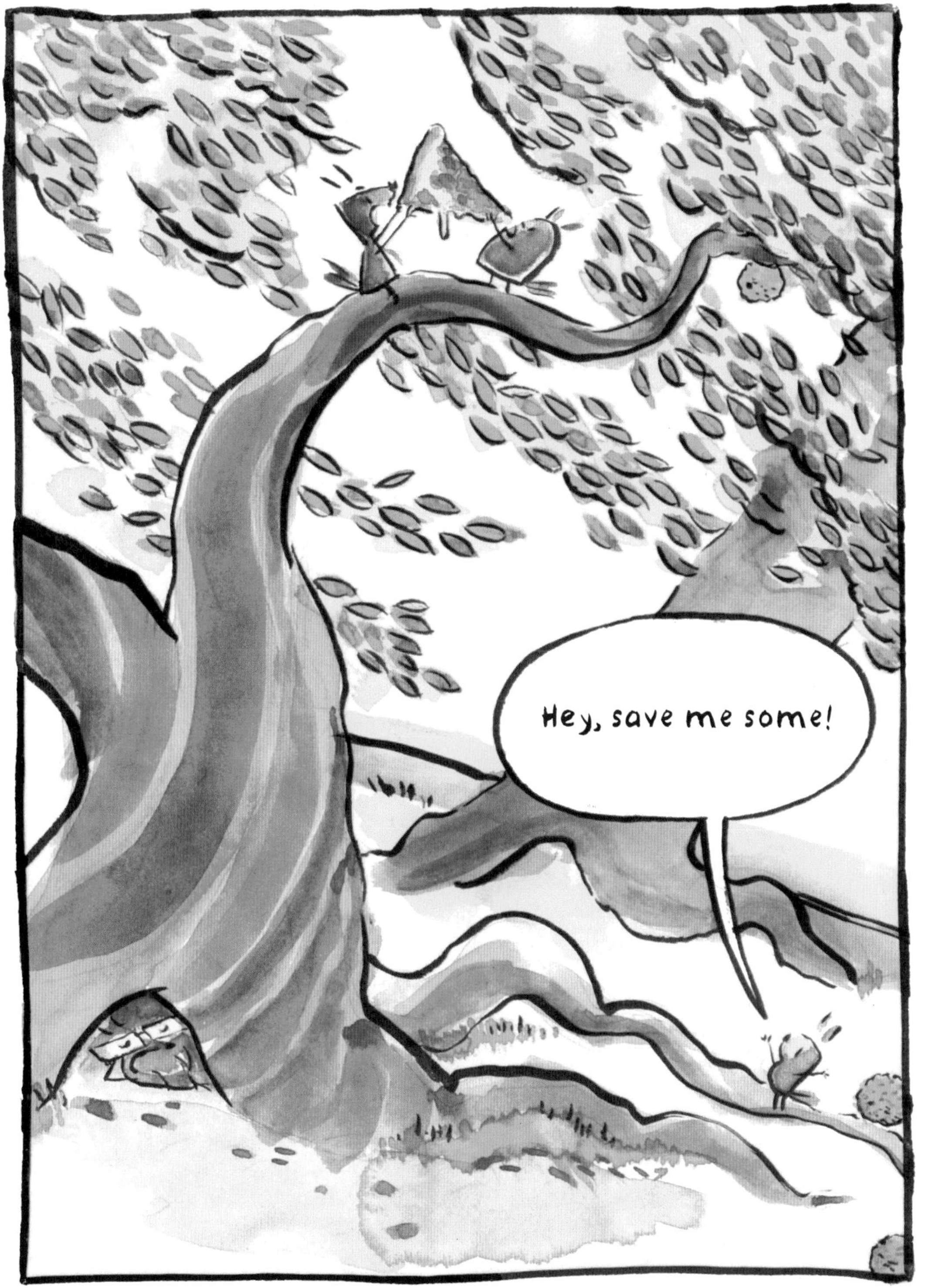
Hey, save me some!

Mika Song is a children's author who makes stories about sweetly funny outsiders. She has illustrated several books including A Friend for Henry by Jenn Bailey, which received a Schneider Family Honor from the American Library Association. She is the creator of the Norma and Belly series, which includes Donut Feed the Squirrels, an Eisner Award nominee, and Apple of My Pie.

She loves drawing on paper and meeting young readers. Her favorite pizza is the one she is about to put in her mouth.

🐦 📷 @mikasongdraws
mikasongdraws.com